CRIMSON BOND

CRIMSON BOND

A DYSTOPIAN VAMPIRE FANTASY ROMANCE

AMY PATRICK

Oxford South Press

CONTENTS

ABOUT

CRIMSON BOND

I never thought I'd see her again. Never dared to hope. But against all odds, Abigail's back. Unfortunately she's as sweet as ever and even more beautiful.

And I'm in serious trouble.

I've learned to hate her in the time she's been away, but the blazing attraction between us is still there. And now, having her close enough to touch—close enough to taste—I'm in a literal battle for my life.

Because my Bloodbound oath still holds, and the punishment for breaking it is still death.

The last thing I want is "alone time" with her, but that's exactly what I get when the queen sends me on a mission, and the only way to keep Abbi alive is to take her with me.

In this third book of the Crimson Accord series, the rift between humans and vampires widens, the menace of the

Crimson Court intensifies, and the temptation for Reece and Abigail grows to a fever pitch.

Will they give in to it? Or will the dangerous secrets that stand between them destroy their chance of love and any hope of living in peace?

Sign up now for Amy Patrick's VIP List and get a free book, exclusive content, and other fun freebies, plus book and sale news!
Join the VIP list here: https://bit.ly/APsVIPs

Keep in touch with Amy Patrick on Facebook, TikTok, Instagram, Goodreads, Bookbub, and Pinterest!

The Crimson Accord Series
Crimson Born
Crimson Storm
Crimson Bond
Crimson Crown

And don't miss The Hidden Saga, Amy's bestselling YA fantasy series. Book 1, Hidden Deep, is free for a limited time on all ebook retailers.

The Hidden Saga
Hidden Deep (FREE ebook)
Hidden Heart
Hidden Hope
The Sway (FREE when you join my list!)
Hidden Darkness (Dark Court, 1)
Hidden Danger (Dark Court, 2)
Hidden Desire (Dark Court, 3)

MIDNIGHT DRIVE

Reece

Running through the hills above the Bastion, I navigated trees and rocky terrain and a few patches of snow left over from the last storm.

It was my nightly routine—rain, shine, or sleet. I wasn't doing it for the mountaintop view, so the weather was of no consequence.

Rather than admiring the natural beauty of Northwestern Virginia, I kept my eyes down and focused on the burn in my leg muscles, the cold air moving in and out of my lungs, pushing my body as hard as possible.

Not only was it good training, it was the only way I could manage to quiet my mind and keep from thinking.

I'd been going for two hours at a punishing pace before I paused to catch my breath and look up. There was a full moon.

A bittersweet pang echoed through my chest in the empty space where I used to have a heart. Technically, I supposed it was still there, but it never beat anymore.

Not since Abbi left.

I'd been so sure it had meant something monumental, meeting her that night with the mysterious crimson moon coloring the sky.

Practically floating to my car after she'd left with her friends, I was already anticipating seeing her again and getting to know her better. I was almost back to the athletic dorm on the HACC campus when it hit me—I should have gotten her address or at least the name of her village. Amish villages were a dime a dozen around there in rural Pennsylvania.

Instead, I'd left it up to "destiny." What a dope.

It was late, but I'd pulled off at an exit and turned the car around. Abbi and her friends were traveling by horse-drawn buggy. They couldn't have gotten that far. I planned to intercept them on the highway and get her contact information—no doubt under the glare of her little wannabe boyfriend.

Backtracking toward the party, I kept my eyes peeled for lamplight or the orange reflective triangle stickers that marked the traditional Amish vehicles. The two-lane highway was straight and empty—extraordinarily dark, too.

After a few miles, my lids began to sag. I'd gotten up early, worked out hard, then stayed at the party far too late. *Worth it.*

And it would certainly be worth this midnight drive when I secured Abbi's address—and her promise to see me again—soon.

Blinking hard and rolling down my windows to let in the cool night air, I focused on staying awake and finding the buggy. I was nearly back to the Miller farm now.

Maybe I'd passed them without noticing? Those Amish buggies were hard to see at night. Hopefully hers hadn't turned off on a side road already.

Damn, this road is dark.

I leaned over the steering wheel, searching the blackness. A vision of Abbi's pretty face filled my mind. The fullness and natural berry color of her lips. Her shy green eyes that held an alluring spark of strength and strong will.

And then the beautiful picture had been shredded by noise and sickening motion and flames. I'd awakened to find myself hanging upside down by my seatbelt, the windows and windshield of my Dodge Charger Hellcat obliterated, and the ominous smell of hot motor oil mixed with the scent of blood.

That was the totality of my memories until I woke up again in my parents' backyard. What happened after that I'd rather not remember. I wasn't sure how I'd even made it the next few months until I'd been captured and brought to the Bastion.

That was when life had begun again. Because of Abbi and her unshakable conviction that I was worth saving. She'd been wrong, but God love her for believing it.

Of course in the end, she'd realized the truth, and she'd left. Now we had our own separate lives—hers as an activist for the Vampire-Human Coalition, promoting peace, and mine as a member of the Bloodbound, preparing for war.

I started back down the mountain toward the Bastion where I would join my brothers and the recruits who'd been assigned to me for our nightly drills. They were the only family I had left, and I was grateful for them. But I didn't feel the way they all seemed to about the job.

They talked about the adrenaline rush of using their enhanced strength and skills, the pulse-pounding excitement of the hunt. My pulse never pounded—not anymore. In fact, the only times I'd really felt alive since turning were the times I'd spent alone with Abbi.

Those days were long gone. I'd likely never see her again —unless we happened to bump into each other when I went out to LA on my mission. There was an annoying flutter in my chest at the thought of it.

It had been several days since I'd proposed the idea to Imogen, but she still hadn't given me the go ahead to start my journey to the West Coast and the Vampire-Human Coalition headquarters.

When I neared the entrance to the caverns, I spotted two young females running toward it. Were they just playing around or were they in some sort of trouble?

My Bloodbound training kicked in, and I scanned the surrounding area, searching for someone chasing them or any other potential threat. They seemed to be alone.

And then I realized who they were. All the air left my lungs. It was Heather and Kelly, Abbi's friends who'd left for California with her. What were they doing here?

Is she with them?

Again, I surveyed the Bastion's above-ground property. No. She wasn't with them.

Why not?

Picking up speed, I intercepted them before they entered the cavern. "Kelly. Heather. What are you doing here? What's happened?"

Something had definitely happened. They both looked disheveled, not to mention strangely dressed—in Amish clothing—and they wore matching expressions of panic.

"It's Abbi," the small blonde one—Kelly—said between sucking breaths. Apparently they'd been running for quite a distance. "She's hurt."

"Where is she?" I demanded. "California?"

Heather answered, also breathing hard. "No. She's at the state line checkpoint on I-81. About thirty-five miles north of here. The border agent called in police backup when he figured out we were wanted. Abbi tried to save us, and he shot her. He said it was an exploding platinum round. She told us to make a run for it."

Shit. This was bad. Those rounds were the latest and greatest anti-vamp weapon, and vampire haters loved them for a reason. They worked.

For a second I debated the best course of action. As fast as I was, one of our Bloodbound vehicles would still be faster. Kannon was already out on patrol with a group.

Were all of the vehicles out? I'd have to run down the street to our parking area, but no—I needed to go into the caverns first and grab some keys.

Before I could do either, a Bloodbound soldier named Tyrone emerged from the cavern's entrance. He was one of the queensguard, Imogen's personal protection unit, of which I was captain.

Our eyes locked. "Good, you're back," he said. "I was afraid I was going to have to track you down on your nightly trek through the mountains."

"I've already heard. I was about to go to the scene."

Now his face scrunched in confusion. "The scene? I was looking for you to tell you Imogen has summoned you. She said it's of utmost importance and wants to see you in her chambers immediately."

2

A CLOSE CALL

Reece

Clenching my fists at my sides, I blew out a breath of barely controlled frustration.

If it was so important for me to get to that checkpoint, why would Imogen insist on seeing me first? Every second that passed was one I *wasn't* spending helping Abbi. Maybe our queen wasn't aware of what was going on above ground tonight.

"There's been an incident at a nearby checkpoint," I said to Tyrone, glancing toward the road and fighting to stay in place instead of running toward it.

"There'll be an incident *here* if you refuse the queen's summons—a beheading," he warned. "Kannon and his team are on their way to the checkpoint. He'll handle whatever's happening there."

So she *did* know. And he was right. To disobey the queen was certain death.

I almost didn't care. Every fiber of my being burned to go to Abbi.

How badly was she injured? What was she doing so close to the Bastion? Had she been on her way here? She knew better. If the platinum bullet didn't kill her, Imogen would.

Which was why I nodded and followed Tyrone inside. I was no good to Abbi dead. Alive, I could at least intercede with Imogen if necessary.

Maybe that was what the queen's summons was about. Perhaps she intended to send me to the scene. It would be a small delay, but I'd simply drive that much faster.

I ran through the caverns and corridors to the queen's private chambers. Obviously I was expected because the soldiers guarding the door stepped aside. I knocked and entered, forgetting to wait for her invitation.

Imogen sat at an antique vanity table, brushing her hair. She wore a deep red silk dressing gown loosely tied at the waist so it gaped open at the top to expose her cleavage.

Seeing me in the mirror, she turned slowly to face me. A smile spread across her red lips.

"It's a good thing you're my favorite. Anyone else who entered my chambers without permission would find himself lacking a head."

I bowed stiffly, struggling to contain my impatience. "Forgive me, my queen. I was told you needed to see me immediately on a matter of great importance. I was in a hurry."

Her smile widened. "Yes, and I know *why* you're in such a hurry. Your eagerness to obey me has nothing to do with it. Never fear, your friend Kannon is taking care of the situation at the checkpoint. He's transporting the girl here."

"Where? To the medical clinic?"

I prepared to turn and run toward the place I'd spent so much time when I'd first arrived at the Bastion, when *I* was the one in bad shape and Abbi had saved *my* life.

Imogen's pleasant smile turned savage. "I will make sure you're informed of her whereabouts—*after* you've done what I require of you."

Oh God no. Not now.

Not *ever* would be preferable, but honestly, Imogen couldn't expect me to "serve" her at a moment like this, could she?

She'd never summoned me to her chambers for that reason, but I knew from the other guys what happened in this room. It would be *so* like her to claim her rights with me when Abbi was on her way back to the Bastion. When my heart was so close to returning to my chest.

Frankly, she was going to be disappointed. There was no way I'd be able to summon the necessary "enthusiasm" to get the job done.

Imogen laughed. It was not a jovial sound. "You should see your face. What *can* you be thinking? Perhaps it's a good thing I don't share my sister's gift of intuition. I doubt I'd like what I'd see in your head right now."

She stood and moved away from the vanity table toward her enormous walk-in closet.

"As for what I require of you... I need you to go to the armory and count the weapons for me."

I didn't follow her, frozen in place by shock. "Count the weapons?"

Was she joking? Abbi was out there hurt, possibly dying, and she was assigning me a task that could easily have been performed by the most junior member of our ranks.

Her voice from inside the closet sounded blasé. "Yes, the daggers and swords and various types of guns. Armor too. I want to know how much we have of each sort and what kind of condition it's in."

Frustration and impatience simmered in my veins, raising

them precariously close to the surface. This was the definition of busywork. I went to the closet door but didn't enter, summoning all my reserves of self-discipline to keep my tone measured and respectful.

"My queen, I can assign someone to—"

Imogen whirled to face me, her acidic tone cutting me off sharply. "I don't want *someone*. I want *you*. You're the only one I trust to give me an accurate count."

She turned back to browsing through a rack of hanging dresses, all black. "When you are finished with that, *then* you may find Kannon and inquire about your childhood sweetheart's condition—assuming she lives long enough to even reach our sanctuary."

Glancing back over her shoulder, she gave me a cheeky grin then dropped the dressing gown. "I hope she does. I have *plans* for her. It would be such a shame if she died prematurely. You are dismissed."

Seething and gritting my teeth, I bit out, "Yes, my queen," turned, and left her chambers.

My bond of fealty to her had chafed since the moment I'd accepted it—but never so much as in this moment. Now it felt like a chain of molten silver was wrapped around my neck, scorching and choking me as I walked toward the armory.

It was nearly impossible to keep my attention trained on the task. On the other hand, I needed to finish it as quickly as possible so I could respond when Kannon radioed that he'd arrived with Abbi.

He *would* inform me, wouldn't he? *Of course he will.* He had to know I'd be... interested.

When the call came over my walkie, Kannon didn't address me by name, but his announcement grabbed every ounce of my attention. There was no one in this place—or anywhere in the world for that matter—who cared more about what he had to say in this moment.

"I'm in house—on my way to the clinic," he said. "If anyone's near there, let Dr. Coppa know we're gonna need a lot of O-neg blood. I've got a gunshot victim here who's about to bleed out."

A sword of icy fear gutted my mid-section. The physical one I was holding dropped to the floor with a clatter, and I took off in a full sprint down the west corridor toward the cavern that housed the medical center.

I made it to the clinic before Kannon did. Where *was* he?

If Abbi was that badly in need of blood, why wasn't he moving faster? I was about to go searching for him when I spotted him coming down the dark corridor. In his arms, he carried a limp figure.

Oh God. No. Please no.

The body in his arms looked lifeless. The sword in my gut twisted and sank in deeper. But no, Abbi had to be still alive —she wouldn't need blood if she were dead.

And I could *feel* her somehow.

I stepped into the center of the corridor, intending to take her from Kannon and carry her into the clinic myself. If she really was dying, if these were her last moments, *I* wanted to be the one holding her.

And I needed to finally tell her the truth.

She might not be able to hear me. Maybe she wouldn't even care about hearing it anymore—she'd moved on with her life. But for my own sanity, I couldn't let her leave this world without ever saying it out loud.

Someone stepped out from behind Kannon, and my heart nearly sprang from my chest.

Abbi.

Confusion battled with elation inside me as I realized the person in Kannon's arms was not her but someone else.

And then I smelled him. A male. A *human* male. *What the...*

At the moment I couldn't be bothered to wonder about his identity because Abbi had stopped in place, returning my stare. She was disheveled, covered in blood, and... stunning.

The night we'd met, I had thought she was the greatest natural beauty I'd ever seen. The lustrous, dark hair, the huge, innocent eyes, and tempting full lips that seemed more fitting for a model than an Amish farmgirl. She'd been completely unaware of her appeal, which had only made her *more* appealing.

Seeing her now after making do with my memories and imagination for so long was almost overwhelming.

My heart, which hadn't moved since the day she'd left, gave a hard thump. My eyes drank in the sight of her, scanning from the top of her bonnet-covered head to the familiar plain black boots. There was blood on her long skirt.

From the scent of it, it was a mixture of hers and the human's. I couldn't care less about his condition, but at least hers didn't seem to be serious. She was walking on her own and didn't appear to be in pain.

"Hello Reece." She sounded out of breath—from the walk through the caverns? From her injury? From the shock of seeing me?

I was battling a bout of breathlessness myself. But I didn't want her to see that. If she wasn't dying, there was no need for a deathbed confession from me. I worked to master my expression and hide my reaction to seeing her again.

Lifting my chin, I gave her a smirk. "I see reports of your demise were somewhat premature. Heather and Kelly said you'd been shot. They said it was an exploding round."

"Yes. I... I guess it was only a flesh wound. A close call."

My pulse settled then skyrocketed again as my gaze fell on her necklace—the pendant I'd given her the day she'd left.

She was still wearing it. It was broken. And empty. Was *that* how she'd survived the bullet?

My gaze flew up to meet hers again. The confirmation was there in her eyes—or at least I thought it was.

If it *was* my blood that had saved her life, I was glad. I was also screwed.

3

MILLION-DOLLAR QUESTION

Reece

Imogen would kill me if she knew I'd given my blood to Abbi. She'd probably kill her too.

In fact, Abbi's life was in danger just for coming here. Why the hell had she returned? Did she not value her own life at all?

She'd said there was nothing here for her and made it quite clear *I* wasn't enough reason to stick around.

If it weren't for Kannon standing there, I would have ordered her to turn around and leave the Bastion. As it was, he—and probably all the members of his team—had seen her already. Imogen wouldn't be satisfied until she'd seen Abbi herself.

And dealt with her.

"What *can* you be thinking coming back here?" I growled at her.

The question came out more harshly than I'd intended, and the look on Abbi's face told me it had stung her. But her expression morphed quickly into fiery defiance.

"Well, it's nice to see you, too. The Bastion is a refuge for vampires in trouble, is it not? I'm in trouble. I didn't know where else to go."

Not what I'd been expecting, but I supposed it made sense. Abbi wasn't stupid. And of course she wouldn't risk coming back here unless she'd literally had no other choice.

The spark of idiotic hope that had sprung to life inside me died in a pile of black, smoldering ash.

"What kind of trouble?" I demanded.

"My friends and I are wanted by the authorities."

What could a peace-loving former Amish girl possibly have done to run afoul of the human police? I glanced over at the unconscious human male. He was young, about our age. This had to be about him somehow.

"Friends?" I scoffed. "All I see is a half-dead human."

Abbi's voice turned acidic. "I meant Kelly and Heather. And yes, Shane *is* my friend. And yes, he's a human—who's hurt as you can see. He needs immediate medical attention, so if you'll please let us pass..."

She looked at me, brows raised expectantly.

Shane. Her friend.

Who was this guy? Had she found him on the road somewhere? Or had he come with her from California?

Was he *more* than a friend, as in a... a boyfriend?

How dare she bring him here. How dare she risk her own life for a human. She was too nice. He'd never do the same for her.

I did not move to let them pass. "Still a human-loving do-gooder, I see. That doesn't explain why you brought him here. If his injuries don't kill him, which based on the smell of things they will, then some thirsty Bastion citizen will do the job. Probably the good doctor himself. Either way, I seriously doubt Shawn will make it through the night."

"His name is *Shane*—and I'm going to at least try to save him. Unlike you, I don't give up on the people I care about."

Abbi hadn't raised a hand to me, but I felt as if I'd been slapped. It was hard to say which hurt more—her admission that she cared for him—or her accusation that I hadn't cared *enough* about her.

Everything I'd done had been about her. She was the reason I'd sacrificed *everything.*

Fury and jealousy whirled together in an emotional tornado, dislodging my self-control and sending my rational thought spinning. My hands moved without my permission, gripping her small shoulders, pulling her close. I glared down into her upturned face.

"If you've fallen in love with this weak human, you're even more foolish than I thought you were. Whether he lives or dies, it won't last, you know."

Not the least bit intimidated, Abbi jutted out her stubborn little chin. "My feelings for him are none of your business. You made sure of that when you took the Bloodbound vows. Now please let us by."

My feelings for him. My feelings for him. My feelings for him.

The phrase ricocheted through my brain, echoing to its borders, leaving a wake of pain.

Kannon's voice broke through the tumult. "Yeah dude— this kid's skinny, but he's got heavy bones or something."

Nodding numbly, I let out my pent-up breath and stepped out of the way. Before the three of them disappeared into the clinic, I gathered myself enough to issue a clipped order.

"Get him settled and come right back out. I'm supposed to take you to Imogen."

It wasn't strictly true. Imogen hadn't ordered *me* to bring Abbi to her, but she'd definitely summon her at some point, and I wanted to be there when the two of them stood face-to-face again.

Hopefully Imogen would simply remind her she wasn't

welcome and tell her to get lost. I'd escort Abbi to the exit and once again, let her go for her own good. And for mine.

That was the best case scenario. What was I going to do if the worst case happened? I was still stewing over it when Abbi re-emerged from the clinic. We walked toward the throne room together in tense silence.

My mind crackled with all the things I wanted to say, wanted to *ask*—about the human and her life since we'd last seen each other, and what had happened to her at the checkpoint. But if I asked, it might seem like I cared, and I couldn't *let* myself care.

Not when she'd only be leaving again.

She didn't come back for you. Remember that.

She was the one who ended the silent standoff. "You haven't said anything about the fact I broke the pendant and drank your blood."

So my blood *had* saved her. And I had indeed broken my vows to Imogen.

The fact I'd committed a deadly offense did nothing to quell the ridiculous joy surging inside me. Ridiculous because it wasn't like Abbi and I had mated or something.

But we had shared blood. Maybe *that* was how I'd known Abbi was still alive.

I kept my response as nonchalant as possible. "Your leg is covered in blood. Your blood. So I'm assuming the gunshot didn't graze you but penetrated your leg. Which means you did what you had to do." I shrugged. "It was an emergency. That's why I gave it to you—in case of emergency."

Total lie, but if I'd anticipated the possibility of her ever being shot, I *would* have given it to her for that reason.

"Is that the only reason?"

Damn, the girl was a mind reader. I shot her a panicked side glance. Wait—was she? No, she looked like she was genuinely wondering, not calling me on my bullshit.

"What other reason would there be?"

Abbi waited a beat before responding, and she didn't answer my question. *Thank God.*

"Why are you angry I've come back?"

Ah. The million-dollar question. One with too many answers. They banged around in my brain like sneakers in a dryer.

Because I hate you for leaving.

Because I still love you.

Because you love someone else.

Because I'm afraid you're going to die for it.

I ended up giving her none of them. Instead, I said, "I'm not angry. I have no particular feelings about it whatsoever."

How many lies could I tell in a single conversation? Apparently, I was going for a record. The truth would get us *both* executed, so I kept going.

"I'm merely curious... as to what could have made you think this place is safer for you than the outside world. Than *anywhere* else in the world."

The pain in her eyes surprised me. Did she want me to be happy she was back here, putting her life in danger?

"Believe me, I never intended to come back," she said. "I'm well aware no one wants me here. What can I say? I was desperate."

Right. She hadn't come back for me. She was here for Imogen's protection and help. Poor kid.

She shouldn't get her hopes up for that.

4

WRONG ANSWER

Reece

"You should know, things have changed since you left," I said.

"Oh really? So you're *not* Imogen's whipping boy, indulging her every whim these days?"

Oh, that sassy little mouth. How I wanted to shut it up. A vivid memory seized my brain—the two of us locked in a desperate kiss in that dark alcove at the Inception Ball.

No. Stop. Never ever ever *happening again so don't even think it.*

I shook my head and bit the inside of my cheek to dispel the dangerous image. "Our population has exploded since President Parker took office. More and more vampires are losing their jobs, their homes. Many are being imprisoned on false charges."

"Tell me about it," Abbi muttered.

Sounded like the voice of experience. What *had* happened to drive her back to this place when, as she'd said, she'd never intended to return?

"You said you were in trouble. What happened?"

"I'll explain it all to your queen when we see her. No point in telling the story twice."

Okay then. She didn't want my concern. She needed my warning though, whether she realized it or not.

"Most of all, Imogen has changed," I told her. "She's less patient than she used to be with the way things are going in the outside world."

Abbi gasped. "*Less* patient? Is that even possible?"

"You'll see. She's no longer content to sit idly by in the safety of our stronghold while, out in the world, the injustices against our species multiply."

"I can hardly believe I'm saying this, but I sort of agree with her," Abbi said. "Maybe peace at any cost *isn't* the answer. But I'm not sure what the answer is. What is she planning to do?"

"I'm not at liberty to talk about it. She'll share that with you if she chooses to," I said as we reached the throne room chamber.

Standing before the heavy iron doors, I was suddenly gripped with a fierce impulse to snatch Abbi up and whisk her to the surface, to get her as far away from this place—and from Imogen—as possible before it was too late.

But then, it was already too late.

"You remember your court etiquette, don't you?" I asked.

"Of course. Bow, address her as 'my queen,' don't piss her off and get myself beheaded. It hasn't been *that* long since I was here."

I stared down into Abbi's far-too-innocent eyes, anxiety twisting in my mid-section.

"You don't think so? Feels like an eternity to me."

The doors to the throne room opened, and the guards stood back to let us pass. As we made our way toward the front of the room where Imogen sat, the other queensguard gave me nods of respectful acknowledgment.

In the past year, I'd risen to the position of captain. My duties kept me here most of the time instead of out on patrols. The guys in this unit were good men, and I did my best to keep them out of Imogen's crosshairs and in her good graces.

Working this closely with her every day, there was the constant threat of tripping her wires and setting off her mercurial temper. Her queensguard took the brunt of it.

There was a decent crowd in the room. Supplicants were lined up to seek Imogen's intervention in some matter or another—or to plead for her mercy if they'd run afoul of Bastion rules.

She wore her usual bored expression as she listened to the couple at the front of the line. Observing her from across the room, I supposed she might have appeared beautiful to a casual onlooker. The outer hallmarks of great beauty were all there.

But I knew her insides. No matter what she wore or how she styled her hair and makeup, Imogen's looks did nothing for me.

She ignored our entrance, but naturally she was aware of it. Finally, she glanced in our direction, and I bowed deeply.

"My queen."

Beside me, Abbi's heart rate and breathing quickened. She was scared. In spite of my best efforts to contain it, sympathy for her surged in my chest and made me want to step in between the two women.

Imogen stood and dismissed her waiting subjects. No doubt they were disappointed, but no one said a word as the queensguard escorted them from the room.

Two of the guards stayed with Imogen as she approached us. I didn't like the look on her face. Not sure what I'd expected, but this wasn't it.

She looked pleased to see Abbi—a little too pleased.

"I knew you'd be back," Imogen said. "You have a lot of nerve showing your face here again after such betrayal, little one."

Sensitive to their queen's tone, the guards flanking her gripped their daggers and prepared to strike at her command. My own hands shook with the effort to keep from reaching for my weapon.

I should never have brought Abbi here. Any moment now Imogen would order one of them—or maybe even me—to execute her.

And I'd be faced with an impossible decision—keep my Bloodbound vows and let it happen, or...

"I never meant to betray you. I was simply following my conscience," Abbi said. Her voice was remarkably composed. "I know you didn't want me to return, but I didn't see another choice."

She continued to calmly explain what had happened to her and her friends, how they were falsely arrested and imprisoned in one of those so-called Safety Centers.

Hmmph. More like concentration camps. We'd heard about some of the things being done to vampires in those places. It was one of the reasons for the increase in our Bloodbound recruiting efforts.

My blood boiled at the thought of Abbi in prison. Imogen didn't seem surprised though. Had she been aware all along her daughter was incarcerated and had done nothing?

It seemed likely, considering her mocking tone. "Did your dear Sadie do nothing to help free you?"

"I'm sure she would have if she'd known where we were or what had happened to us," Abbi said. "When we escaped, I was unable to reach her. There was an attack on the Vampire-Human Coalition headquarters. It's been destroyed."

What? When had *that* happened?

Was this why Imogen had delayed approving my mission to go to Sadie and convince her to join the vampire resistance?

"I heard about that. Pity," the queen said.

So it wasn't a surprise to her, as it was to me. Why hadn't I been told? Maybe Imogen didn't consider it need-to-know information for the captain of her personal guard.

Or maybe she'd suspected that if I'd heard about the attack on the VHC headquarters, I'd have left for LA with or *without* her permission.

Seething, I tried to focus on the rest of their conversation. I needed to remain alert to Imogen's signals, to determine her intentions toward Abbi.

She was asking questions, at least feigning interest in why her daughter had returned. Apparently Abbi and her friends had escaped the Safety Center somehow and several humans had been killed in the process. Now the girls were wanted by federal authorities.

Imogen seemed to find it all very amusing. She smiled. "So... you've come back to my court to beg for my protection. Perhaps you have a better understanding now of my feelings toward humans—and my disdain for my sister's approach to dealing with their species."

"In spite of what happened to me, I still believe in Sadie's teachings," Abbi said. "I still believe in peace."

Oh no. Wrong answer.

Now my hand did grip my dagger blade, anticipating Imogen's kill order.

5
SMALL ALTERATION

Reece

Grabbing one of her guards' daggers, Imogen stabbed *him* with it, plunging the blade into his thigh.

"How can you still be so naïve?" she yelled at Abbi. "They locked you up, hunted you—*my* daughter. It's an outrage. There can *be* no peace with them."

Still trembling with adrenaline, I eased my hand away from my weapon before Imogen took notice. She *was* angry with Abbi, but she'd taken it out on the poor soul suffering in silence beside her instead of on her daughter.

As for Abbi, she was clearly shaken. Her eyes were wide and dark, and her voice quivered.

"They're not all bad. There's a human boy who risked his life to help us get here. Shane. He took a bullet for me."

It was my turn to be angry. There was only one reason the human would have done that. He was in love with her. I couldn't prevent the low, involuntary growl that came out.

"Yes, I'm aware of that too," Imogen said with apparent amusement. "In fact, when I was informed you brought him *with you*—to *my* court—I almost didn't believe it. You're still capable of surprising me, little one. I'm told you actually asked our medical personnel to save his life."

When she told Abbi how pointless it was, that she couldn't allow the human to leave here alive, Abbi said, "You're going to have him killed?"

She actually seemed shocked. She really was still naïve and innocent.

"Unless you'd prefer to turn him," Imogen said.

Ah. That's what this was about. It was the reason Imogen had stabbed Ciprian with his own dagger instead of stabbing Abbi. She saw this as another opportunity to get Abbi to accept her destiny.

If Abbi accepted, the human male would be connected to her for eternity. They'd share an unbreakable bond, and *he* wasn't Bloodbound.

Another growl surfaced.

Abbi wore a tortured gaze, begging Imogen not to force her into turning Shane. So she *didn't* want that kind of bond with him. For a moment, I was happy. Until she spoke again.

"I'd rather die myself."

No. The last thing she should have been doing was putting homicidal ideas into Imogen's head. Or challenging her orders. But she *had* done it, and the queen appeared all too ready to take her up on her challenge.

"Very well," Imogen said. "It will sadden me, but my primary responsibility as queen is protecting our people against any and all threats. The needs of the many outweigh the needs of the few."

She turned to Mason, the uninjured guard. "Seize her. Put her in a holding cell. We'll have a public assembly in the Great Dome tomorrow night."

She was going to kill her. In front of everyone.

Before I even realized what I intended to do, my feet moved, and I stepped forward.

"No."

Realizing I'd directly interfered with the queen's order—a deadly offense—I dropped to one knee and bowed my head. My brain scrambled for a way to save Abbi and myself.

"My queen, I think I may have a better solution, if you'll allow me to speak."

I felt her fingers on my head, the long nails delving beneath my hair to my scalp. A shiver of disgust went down my spine as it always did when she touched me.

If Imogen was aware of it, she didn't care. Her tone was equal parts loving and menacing. "Of course you may speak. You *are* my favorite queensguard. You may rise."

I stood and presented the strategy that had popped into my mind fully formed. "I see this as a great opportunity, my queen. Abigail could be useful on the mission you've assigned me."

She smirked. "You mean the mission *you* proposed and I approved. Yes, go on."

"She can get close to Sadie like no one else. Spare her life, and I will personally supervise her to make sure she follows your orders and doesn't get into more trouble." *And I can get her away from here, far from your reach.* "You can keep the human male here as... motivation."

"Wait," Abbi said. "What is this 'mission?'"

Imogen and I both ignored her. I knew the queen regarded the human male's life as disposable, but he was clearly important to Abbi. Which Imogen now realized, thanks to my suggestion. Hopefully she'd consider him a strong enough bargaining chip to let us leave together.

Imogen turned to Abbi. "Reece has suggested, quite wisely, that there is strength in numbers. We are strong here at the Bastion, but there aren't enough of us to wage war on the entirety of the human race. We need to bring vampire-kind together under united leadership. Even before the attack on the VHC, Reece volunteered to go to my sister and convince her of this fact."

Now she glanced back and forth between us with a calculating gleam in her eyes. "He's quite right. Sadie's fondness for you will make her more receptive to meeting with him and listening to what he has to say. I'll allow it."

The battle-ready tension drained from my body, leaving my limbs shaky and suddenly fatigued.

"Thank you, my queen. I believe that is a wise choice."

"Let's hope Abigail is wise in *her* choices. Remember, little one, as you go out into the world again tomorrow and reunite with your beloved 'leader,' that I have your friend Shane."

Abbi looked ready to cry. "Please don't hurt him," she begged. "He doesn't deserve it."

Imogen dismissed us, and I escorted Abbi to the secure chambers where she'd spend the day sleeping before we left tomorrow night.

Once she was safely inside, I returned to the throne room.

"I'm surprised to see you back here. And so soon," Imogen quipped. "I would have thought you'd be guarding every step the little princess took to make sure she didn't stumble."

I bowed. "My duty is to you and only you, my queen."

The truth was I hadn't wanted to leave Abbi, even behind a locked door. There were grumbles among some of Imogen's loyalists that the "traitor" should never have been allowed to take a step inside the stronghold ever again. I was worried someone might take it upon himself to prove his devotion to the queen by taking her out.

But the greatest threat to Abbi's life was standing in front of me. I'd be a fool to let her know I had any remaining feelings for her daughter.

"When I said you were dismissed, I meant for the rest of the night," the queen clarified. "You'll need to rest and prepare for your trip. I am glad you've returned for the moment, though. There's something I wanted to discuss with you in private before you leave."

"Yes, my queen? What is it?"

"There's been a small... *alteration* to your mission. Send everyone else out of the room, and I'll fill you in on the details."

6

FANTASIES OF BLOODSHED

Reece

I spent the rest of the night and daylight hours outside the entrance to Abbi's room.

Imogen had sent me away to get some sleep, but after what she'd told me, sleep wasn't going to happen. I slumped to the floor, resting my back and the top of my head against Abbi's door, listening to the slow and steady rhythm of her breathing.

Why did she have to come back?

Well, I understood why, but things were hopelessly complicated now, and it was partially my fault. While my spontaneous plan to keep Abbi alive had actually worked, the result was I would be spending at least the next few days in exquisite torture, alone in a car—or a hotel room—with her.

And there was no way this was going to end well. Even if I did manage to pull off my mission, keep from breaking my Bloodbound vows along the way, and return to the Bastion with Abbi, the "victory" would be short-lived.

Imogen still wanted what she wanted—world domination and Abbi as her heir.

And Abbi wanted... *him.*

I had the chance to meet the human sonofabitch that night. Much to my annoyance, Abbi insisted on going to check on him at the clinic before we left.

During our walk to the medical wing, she'd referred to Shane as a "friend," but when we got there, she wanted to go into his room alone.

Fat chance. I went with her, promising to stand back and say nothing.

That was easier said than done. She approached his bed with such compassion and concern on her face I almost wished I was the one who'd been wounded. And when she reached out and stroked his arm, it took everything in me not to rip the limb from its puny human socket.

The guy woke, looking around in a daze before focusing on Abbi's face. He looked like he'd been given a prize.

"Abigail. Hi. Are you okay?" he asked.

She inquired about his condition, his pain level, and told him he was not in a hospital but in the vampire stronghold, which of course he should have known nothing about.

How much had she told him? Was it enough to eliminate him for "security reasons?"

No. He was supposed to be Imogen's insurance of Abbi's cooperation on the mission. And Abbi would probably hate me forever if I eviscerated her "friend."

The momentary satisfaction might be worth it, though.

"We're in the vampire place?" the guy asked. "It looks like a hospital room... without windows."

"It's a medical clinic. They treated you last night. They're going to make sure you heal properly and keep you safe until I get back," Abbi said.

At which point, I will make it my next *mission to get rid of you, Shane old boy.*

"Where are you going?" Shane asked, looking like a kid who'd lost his favorite toy.

"I have to leave for a while. I'll be back soon, I promise." Her tone held such warmth I had to fight down another growl.

The human sat up in bed, touching the area of his healed wound. "It doesn't hurt at all."

Obviously Dr. Coppa had treated him with vampire blood. Unless Abbi had given him *hers*.

If that was the case, he was about to need another infusion—a big one. I started toward the bed but stopped short as the stupid human lifted his shirt, showing off his abdominal muscles.

Ha. His physique was nothing compared to that of a vampire male's. To mine.

And yet Abbi had chosen him.

I missed the next part of their conversation. My mind was too occupied with fantasies of bloodshed. I tuned back in as Shane took Abbi's hand inside his. *My* hand moved to my dagger belt.

"I'd never do anything to endanger you," he said in a sappy voice. "You know that."

I snorted in disgust, and Abbi pulled her hand away from him, letting it drop to her side. "I know. And I'll make sure you stay safe, too. That's why I have to leave. I have to go and talk to Sadie."

The human got out of bed. "Great. I'll go with you. When do we leave?"

So he knew about Sadie too? He and Abbi must have spent considerable time together if he knew all the players in the vampire world. Either that or they'd gotten very close very quickly.

Neither possibility made me happy.

Abbi pushed the little upstart back to the bed. Not hard enough in my opinion.

"You can't," she said. "And you shouldn't get up yet. Wait for Dr. Coppa to clear you. You can trust him, by the way. He won't hurt you. He'll keep an eye on you until I return."

Finally Shane seemed to notice my presence. He turned my direction and scanned me up and down, taking in the uniform and the weapon at my side.

That's right buddy. You're going nowhere *with her. And I am.*

"They won't *let* me go with you, will they? Am I... I'm a prisoner."

Abbi apologized, and I moved toward them again as he grabbed both her hands. "You could have turned me. You still could. Then I could come with you. I could help you if you turn me."

She said, "No," before I had a chance to.

"Why not?" he whined. "Think about it. It would be *safer* for me. I'd be like you—and my parents. And they'd have no reason to keep me prisoner here. I'd be free."

Abbi shook her head. "Shane... if I turn you... you'll *never* be free. You don't know what it's like. You would regret your decision."

"Not if I got to stay with you. And it would solve that whole I-can't-date-a-human-guy problem."

I let out another loud snort. This guy was pathetic. There was no way she was romantically involved with him. In fact, she'd apparently given him a lame excuse.

She wasn't attracted to him—she felt sorry for him. I stepped back and leaned against the wall again.

Shane twisted around, following my movement. "You wanna mind your own business buddy? I realize you hate humans, but this has nothing to do with you. Just do your job."

I was off the wall and chest to chest with him in a heartbeat. "My *job*—is keeping the princess safe. I won't let anything get in the way of that—certainly not her *pity* for a weak human."

"Princess?" Shane recoiled from me and looked at Abbi.

"My mom's not only the ruler here, she's sort of... a queen," she said, sounding embarrassed.

"Oh. Wow. Well, I guess that explains your reaction when I kissed you the first time."

Kissed? This pipsqueak had *kissed* her? Outrage rolled through me like thunder before an approaching storm.

Abbi placed a soft hand on my bicep, which was quivering with suppressed energy. "Please. Could you give me a minute to say goodbye? Then we can go."

I stared him down another good five seconds then went to wait at the door for the sickening farewell scene to end.

Shane lowered his voice to a near whisper, but of course I could still hear every word. "You're traveling with *him*? I don't like it."

"Join the club," Abbi said. "He's leading the mission, and I'm going along to assist. Believe me, you don't want to go on this trip, and you *don't* want to turn. You shouldn't get any more involved with this world than you already are. I promised to let you return to your life, and I'll do whatever I have to do to keep that promise."

I smirked at my own reflection in the metal door. Good. She was planning to send him packing when we got back.

Apparently old Shane had other plans. In the reflection, I saw him reach out and hold her face. "You're *part* of my life now. A big part. I don't want to lose you."

I whipped around just in time to see him kiss her. If the door handle hadn't been made of heavy-duty stainless steel, it would have turned to powder in my hand.

Abbi didn't slap him, and she didn't resist. "Why did you do that?"

"You really have to ask?"

"You said you were content with being just friends."

"'Content' is a strong word for it," he said. "'Resigned' is more like it. Go do what you have to do. And when you come back, Abigail, I think we should give it a shot."

I'd heard enough. "Time's up. We need to go."

Abbi twisted to look at me then back to Shane. "Goodbye —for now. I *will* come back and free you."

"I'd rather you came back and kept me." He gave her a dopey smile. "Be safe. I'll be waiting."

I congratulated myself for not hurling all over the pristine stone floor, and Abbi and I left the medical clinic together.

7

TOUGHEN UP

Reece

Abbi didn't mention the kiss, and I didn't intend to, but after several minutes of complete silence I couldn't hold it in any longer.

"So you *are* interested in him."

Clearly she was, which had to be why she was so quiet. Probably reliving the *dreamy* moments of tenderness with her *wonderful* human boyfriend. Gag.

"What does it matter to you?" she snapped. "You knew when you joined the Bloodbound, I'd find someone else eventually. Or did you think I'd stay alone forever, pining away for you?"

Ouch. Of course that wasn't what I'd expected of her. Well... not *forever* anyway. A few decades might have been nice.

"No," I muttered. "But *that* guy? Really? A human?"

She gave me a *duh* expression. "I work for the Vampire-Human Coalition. We're all about vampires and humans getting along."

There it was again, that smart mouth, just begging to be

kissed quiet. And not by *Shane.* I resisted the urge and grunted a sullen reply.

"There *is* no Vampire-Human Coalition anymore."

Abbi looked around, apparently just now noticing where we were. Not heading for the exit but in the tunnel leading to the throne room.

"I thought you were in a hurry to leave," she said.

"I am. But Imogen wants to speak with you first."

"What about?"

She sounded panicked. I wasn't all that comfortable with it myself. Imogen hadn't said why she wanted to see Abbi before we left. The queen didn't take kindly to her guards asking questions—not even me.

"I'm not sure. In spite of your accusation that we're 'close,' she rarely explains herself to me."

"So how many Bloodbound is your *queen* sending along to protect her 'favorite soldier?'" Abby asked in a mocking tone.

Maybe she was just nervous and trying to distract herself. Or maybe she was trying to get a rise out of me. I wasn't going to give her the satisfaction. I'd already embarrassed myself once today by getting up in the human guy's face.

It wasn't like he was my competition. There was no competition. I was Bloodbound and thereby ineligible to claim a mate. Abbi had chosen not to be Imogen's heir and a queen-in-training, which meant she'd taken away even the possibility of a distant future liaison between us.

That still hurt whenever I let myself think about it. I was trapped, and she was free, and it didn't seem to bother her at all. What a fool I was to let it bother me.

"None," I said in answer to her question.

Her eyes went wide. "What? It's just the two of us?"

"Yep. A happy little couple on a cross-country vacation."

Abbi ignored my bitter sarcasm. "I thought you said Imogen considered this mission a top priority."

"She does. And that's why we have to avoid attracting too much human attention. Traveling with a group of Bloodbound wouldn't exactly be subtle."

"Oh."

She was quiet for a minute, perhaps considering all the implications of a road trip alone with me. *I'd* been considering them practically nonstop. Then she looked my way again, surreptitiously running her gaze over my face and body.

Just that subtle glance of interest was enough to set me off. My skin warmed everywhere her eyes landed. God, I was gone for this girl. I hated it.

"Reece... I've been wondering... why *are* you all so... well, you know?"

She was so bashful about asking, I couldn't help cracking a smile. "No. So... what?"

"You know what I'm asking. Why are you all so big? Why do you look so... good?"

My grin spread. She might be into the human, but she *had* been checking me out. My physical reaction went far beyond a grin, but that wasn't something she—or anyone else here at the Bastion—needed to know. I simply answered her question.

"I told you before, we have a special diet."

"Right. You said your blood bags come from a special supply. What's so special about it?"

"It's mixed with Imogen's blood. Which reminds me..." I drew a tiny vial from my pocket.

Before Imogen had dismissed me the second time, she'd handed me a dose of her blood with orders to watch Abbi drink it. It was meant to ensure smooth traveling for us, and she'd told me to give it to Abbi sometime before we left.

Now would be the perfect time. Imogen would know I'd

done as she commanded. Besides, Abbi might refuse to drink it once we'd left this place.

I held the vial out to her. "Drink up."

She took it and held it up to the light, swirling the blood inside.

"Wait... is this Imogen's? I don't want it. This is what keeps all of you loyal to her no matter what. No Kool-Aid for me, thank you."

She tried to hand it back, and I retreated a step, showing her my palms. "Queen's orders. She'll know if you haven't taken it."

"Oh. *That's* why she wants to see me. She should know she doesn't have to force me to go along with the plan. She's holding Shane hostage. I'm not going to let any harm come to him."

"Of course you wouldn't. He's too 'important,'" I snarled. "But I don't think that's it. It probably has more to do with your appearance."

"My appearance?"

She glanced down at herself. "What's wrong with how I look?"

You're perfect.

That's what popped into my head. What came out of my mouth was, "Nothing. You look... fine. It's just we're not going to get very far if you're recognized as a fugitive."

"So, I'll wear a disguise. That's what I did to get out of San Francisco," she argued. *Always so stubborn.*

"You won't need a disguise if you'll just do as you're told and drink that."

She gave the vial another wary glance. "Imogen's blood will change my appearance?"

"Not completely. You'll still look like you, only... more."

As if she needed to be more beautiful. God help me, I was

a dead man. It was Imogen's order though, and if Abbi didn't follow it, we'd never make it out the front door.

"Look, it's your choice, but if you don't drink it, you can't come with me. And if you don't come with me and at least try to help me get through to Sadie, Imogen will have no reason to keep your little human sweetie-pie alive. Old Shane's gonna find himself the main course at dinner tonight because you're squeamish about drinking a little royal blood."

That got through to her. She opened the vial and emptied it. For *his* sake.

"How long does the magic pretty-potion take?" she joked sourly after swallowing.

"You're already—" I stopped myself before I launched into some sort of lovesick ode to her beauty, shifting the focus of my answer. "It'll take a few hours to alter your appearance significantly. And another dose or two to enable you to mesmerize humans."

"What did you say?"

"Mesmerize. Humans," I repeated.

"We can't do that."

"Some of us can. The Bloodbound can."

I'd been amazed the first time I'd used my new ability. It came in very handy whenever nearby human authorities caught wind of our activities or when we needed to cover the tracks and mitigate the damage left behind by a rogue vampire. It would no doubt be invaluable on our upcoming trip.

"Imogen calls it 'The Pull.' I call it useful," I said. "Especially now that cars are checked at every state border. And we'll be crossing quite a few of them in the next few days."

When we reached the throne room, Abbi looked

surprised I wasn't going inside with her. Surprised and scared.

"She wants to see you alone," I explained. "She specifically said she didn't want me there."

"Oh."

The fear in her eyes tugged at my rust-stiffened heartstrings. "It'll be okay," I said softly. "I'll be right here waiting."

Ugh. I sounded exactly like that pathetic, besotted human guy we'd left in the med clinic. I needed to toughen up where Abbi was concerned—and fast.

If I didn't, I wouldn't be able to carry out my mission, and I wouldn't stand a chance of sticking to my rigid Bloodbound vows.

Which meant both of us would end up dead.

8

INEVITABLE

Reece

For the next few minutes, I engaged in some serious self-talk, reminding myself how Abbi had chosen to walk away a year ago when she'd believed it meant never seeing me again.

She knew I could never leave Imogen's service, but that hadn't stopped her from running off to seek peace and love and rainbows.

I recalled that she'd never once sent word back about how she was doing—or inquired about how I was faring. And I reminded myself of how quickly she'd moved on with her life—not to mention that she'd brought *living proof* of that fact with her here to the Bastion.

I'd just met the bastard and nearly punched his lights out.

By the time Kannon came along, the self-talk had done its job and my emotional armor was fully intact. Abbi could ride naked in my passenger seat all the way to the Canadian border, and I wouldn't notice.

Much.

"Hey there. Why you coolin' your heels out here? Mommy put you in time out?" Kannon joked.

"Abbi's in there with her," I said, "getting some last-minute 'advice' before we leave for Canada to find Sadie Aldritch."

"We?" He looked confused. Clearly Imogen hadn't updated him on the situation.

"Yeah. Abbi, uh... she's coming with me."

Kannon's head jerked back like someone had flicked water in his eyes. "What? What are you doing? You're going on a road trip with her, just the two of you? Dude, that's not smart."

My jaw hardened. "It's not a romantic getaway. Abbi's going to help me get to Sadie. It won't be a problem. It's just business. No pleasure involved."

"Yeah right. I've seen you two together, remember? You've got more chemistry than a pharmaceutical plant. I give it two days before you're making blanket forts at the Holiday Inn."

He waggled his eyebrows to indicate "making blanket forts" was a euphemism for something more intimate.

"You'll lose that bet. I'm completely over her," I assured him. "That tends to happen when someone leaves you without a look backward. Besides, I'm Bloodbound now. I'll admit before I took my vows I had some lingering feelings for her. Now I feel nothing, except maybe a desire to punish her."

Kannon's blond brows pulled together. He liked Abbi, or at least he had before she'd left. Just recently he'd reminisced about her like she was the baby sister he never had.

"And exactly how do you intend to do that?" he asked. "I wouldn't like to hear you were cruel to her."

I smiled wickedly. "I won't be cruel. I'll be a pain in the ass. I'm going to be the worst travel companion there ever was. Every mile will be more miserable than the last. I'll prove to her just how little she means to me."

Kannon puckered his bottom lip, raising his brows as if impressed. "You've really given this a lot of thought." Then he smiled again. "Last time I checked, that meant you *did* care about someone."

"Not this time."

"Wow, you really are cold-blooded," he said. "Nothing makes your heart beat anymore. She's gorgeous—even hotter than she used to be. I can't believe it has no effect on you. It almost gave *me* all the feels."

I shot him a murderous glare before I realized he was teasing me.

Kannon laughed. "Completely over her, huh? You may be a grouchy bastard, but I suspect you'd no more hurt a hair on Abbi's head than throw yourself on a solar-charged spear coated in liquid platinum. You still love her, don't you?"

"No, I *did* love her, but I wouldn't want that in my life again, even if it were possible. It hurts too much to love someone so deeply."

"I hate to tell you this, bro, but that's the *only* way to love someone," Kannon said. "That's why it wasn't hard for me to give up on the whole thing and pledge myself to Imogen. I was in love once. She supposedly loved me too, but then my girl left me flat when she found out my paralysis was permanent. Never again, thank you."

"It's a good thing we're both Bloodbound now. Neither of us ever has to bother with love again," I said, and we bumped fists.

Outwardly, I was the picture of composure. Inside, I was shaken by how easily Kannon had seen through me—and how easily Abbi had pulled me back into her orbit.

But what I'd said to him was true. I *didn't* want to ever love anyone the way I'd loved Abbi.

Especially not Abbi. It hurt too much.

She'd moved on, and I'd moved past the need for that

kind of thing in my life.

So why was I so filled with anticipation about our road trip together?

"Well, good luck with your mission," Kannon said, grabbing the handle of the throne room door. "And Reece?"

"Yeah?"

"When it comes to Abbi... my momma always said the most painful thing you could do to your enemies was heap 'burning coals of kindness' on their heads. Think about it."

With a wink, he opened the door and disappeared inside.

* * *

A FEW MINUTES LATER, the doors opened again, and Abbi emerged to find me smiling.

Because I had come up with the perfect punishment for her. I wouldn't be a pain in her royal ass. I wouldn't be cruel.

I would be *amazing*.

I'd be funny, charming, polite, and considerate. I'd heap bucketsful of burning-kindness-coals on her head and make her want me more than I *ever* wanted her.

I would make her fall in love with me again.

And then *I* would break *her* heart.

A tingling sensation spread from my head down to my chest and arms then my legs and feet. I shifted from one foot to the other, too filled with anticipation to stand still.

It wouldn't technically be breaking my Bloodbound vows because I wouldn't make love to Abbi... just... seduce her a little.

"Did someone just tell you a great joke or something?" Abbi asked.

I placed a hand lightly on the small of her back and steered her toward the cavern exit, still smiling. "No. I just saw Kannon. We had a good talk."

"About?"

"Nothing much. Guy stuff."

"But it made you happy?"

My grin stretched farther. *Oh yeah.* "Yes. It. Did."

"Ooookay then."

At her questioning tone and expression, I explained. "Look, I figured some things out when we were talking, okay? Come on, Abbi. I'd think you'd be happy to bid farewell to the cranky S.O.B. you found when you got here."

"I am glad," she said, still sounding unsure. "I mean, it would have been a long drive to Canada otherwise."

"Exactly. As long as we're traveling together, we might as well have a good time, right?"

"Right."

Verbally she was agreeing with me, but her body language said she was waiting for a sneak attack.

The girl was smart. I felt a reluctant sense of pride in her. She'd come a long way since her days as a naïve Amish farmgirl.

But she still couldn't read minds. She couldn't see the dark joy bubbling inside me at this chance to make her suffer. At the promise of sweet revenge.

Later, when the trip was over and I'd left her broken, when she'd realized all the sweet words and chivalrous behavior were nothing but a ruse, she'd hate me.

But then that was inevitable.

Eventually she'd find out the *new* aim of my mission to Canada wasn't to secure Sadie's alliance with the Crimson court for a rebellion.

It was to kill Sadie and take her out of play so Imogen could rule over Sadie's followers and be the sole leader of the vampire species.

It was to destroy everything Abbi believed in.

9

THAT PARTICULAR VOW

For the first couple hours of our drive, I was tense.

Reece's abrupt attitude change had jarred me, even alarmed me. And Imogen's warning about what would happen to the people I cared about if we didn't succeed was still fresh on my mind. But after a while, Reece's good mood started rubbing off on me.

He sang along to the radio and told me stories about some of the funnier things he'd encountered on his Bloodbound missions. Relaxed and charming like this, he was once again the guy I'd met the night of the crimson moon.

Against *that* guy, I had no hope of resistance.

"So, I couldn't help but notice this is a Dodge Charger Hellcat," I said. "Black instead of red, though—very vampish of you. Did you name him?"

"This car's a *she*," he corrected. "I call her... Abigail."

My sharp inhale was audible, even over the music.

Reece shot me a devastating grin. "Just kidding. I haven't actually named her. Why don't you do the honors?"

Still blushing, I turned away from him, pretending to study the sky as I thought of something suitable. "Hmmm... what about... Blackberry?"

"Blackberry? That's lame."

"It is not."

He laughed. "I'm sorry, but it is."

"It's not lame. It's beautiful," I protested. "Blackberry was the name of my favorite cow. I raised her from a calf and bottle fed her because her mom died. I named her Blackberry because, well, she was black and also because she was so sweet."

"Oh now, see? You have to go and make me feel bad. Now I have no choice but to give my badass car a girly name."

"You said she *was* a girl."

"Good point. But she's a tough girl." He caressed the dashboard. "Aren't you, Blackberry? Just listen to that engine roar."

His muscular tanned hand stroking the dark leather was so attractive, I actually felt a little jealous.

Great Abbi. Jealous of a car. Pathetic.

What was truly pathetic was how quickly I'd fallen under Reece's spell again. A few smiles and kind words and I was right back where I'd started with him.

I couldn't let myself fall too deep, though. It would be hard to resist when he was acting like his old self, but it was also pointless. Reece was bound for eternity to Imogen, and I would never do anything to tempt him to break those Bloodbound vows. It would mean death for him—and Shane.

I renewed my own vow to stay strong and keep my mind on the mission. Countless other lives depended on it, including Kelly's and Heather's.

I had been allowed a quick goodbye to them before I left but hadn't been able to tell them anything about where I was going or how long I'd be away. At least I'd had the chance to tell Shane what was going on and assure him I was coming back for him.

"I hope Shane will be okay. He must be incredibly lonely there in the clinic, a single human among thousands of vampires," I mused.

Reece's smile faded, a sullen look taking its place. "He'll be fine. Anyway, that weak human isn't exactly my top priority."

"You used to be one of those, you know. So is your family."

"Don't remind me," he muttered, sliding a glance away from the road to land on my face. "So what's the deal with *Shane* anyway? I suppose you two are in *love* or something."

"I don't actually know him that well," I said honestly.

"You knew him well enough to tell him about Sadie and the Bastion."

"We were traveling together. He was helping us get past the border checkpoints. I had to tell him a little about where we were going and why."

"And you two were on the road together how long?" he asked.

"Three days."

"Three days." He smirked. "And three *nights*."

"It wasn't just the two of us. Kelly and Heather were there, too."

"I didn't hear him asking about Kelly and Heather in the clinic. Seemed pretty damn excited to see you, though."

Reece shot me another side-glance, this one considerably more acidic. "Don't try to tell me nothing happened between you."

I was getting tired of his accusatory tone and the needless third degree. So I said something I probably shouldn't have.

In a tone I probably shouldn't have used.

"I didn't say *nothing* happened."

Clenching the steering wheel in a death grip, Reece whipped the car into the far-right lane then onto an exit ramp. "We need gas," he grunted. "And blood bags."

He practically leapt from the driver's side door after parking at the pump. Jamming the nozzle into the gas tank opening, he left it and stalked into the station's convenience store.

I stayed in the car, heart pumping and working hard to suppress an inappropriate sense of elation. Had I made him jealous? If so, that was *not* a good thing. No matter how good it might feel.

Feelings like that were forbidden for us, though God knew I was jealous of his physical relationship with Imogen.

Nope. Don't go there. Not helpful. Not helpful at all.

When Reece returned to the car, he had visibly calmed. No sign of jealousy or even irritation. Serenity personified. He offered me one of the blood bags he'd purchased and calmly pulled the car back onto the highway.

Either I'd imagined his extreme reaction earlier, or he'd decided to take the same approach I meant to take to this trip. Focus on the mission. Keep emotions in check.

That was the smart thing to do, and for the next few hours we kept our conversation firmly in the safe zone, chatting about the music on the radio and the different states we passed through. I told him a bit about Los Angeles and San Francisco, and we talked about Sadie.

"You will absolutely love her when you meet her," I said. "Everyone does."

"Yeah, okay." His tone was detached. He was probably zoning out from so many hours of driving.

"You want to pull over for a bit and take a break?"

"No, I'm fine. Let's keep going. I want to make it to Buffalo, New York before daybreak," he said. "We're making good time. At this rate we'll make it to Sudbury tomorrow night."

"You know... when we get there and you do meet Sadie, I think you'll find you two have a lot in common. Your leadership styles are similar—commanding but respectful. You both lead by deserving loyalty, not by simply demanding it."

"No offense, but how would you know?" he asked.

"I could tell by the way your men looked at you. And by some things Kannon has said about you."

"Well, I just treat them the way I'd want to be treated."

"Exactly. And that's what Sadie does—with vampires and humans alike."

Imogen couldn't have been any more different from Sadie. And from Reece. She ruled through fear, which never created true loyalty.

"She's going to love you, too," I assured Reece. "In fact, if you ever wanted a change, I know Sadie would love to have you—"

"Stop right there," Reece warned, cutting me off mid-sentence. "Just listening to this is treason."

"It's just the two of us, and we're hundreds of miles from the Bastion. No one there can hear us, not even Imogen."

"It doesn't matter. What I *think* you're suggesting is impossible. You know I took a vow."

"Which means nothing outside the Bastion. There's a whole world out here, Reece."

Being alone with him and seeing him away from the Bastion had shown me the old Reece *was* still in there somewhere. It had created a new spark of hope in me.

And he was right, I *had* been suggesting he leave the Bloodbound behind and join Sadie's efforts. To me it seemed like a great solution, especially now that Imogen was willing to join forces and work with her sister.

"A lot of vampires have never even heard of Imogen," I told him. "They get along just fine without her. You could too. And if you're not *in* the Crimson Court any longer, would she really care that you left the Bloodbound?"

Reaching over with his right hand, Reece literally covered my mouth. "Stop Abbi. It's not going to happen."

"Why not?"

"For one thing, her blood prevents us from disobeying orders."

"Not you. I haven't forgotten how you defied her when she was about to force me to turn that human."

Reece had intervened at the last moment when I'd believed I had no choice in the matter, refusing to abide by the deal I'd made with Imogen to free him from his Bloodbound vows. He'd even drawn his dagger and thrown it between me and the human man—right in front of the queen.

Of course, he'd also said he *wanted* to be Bloodbound even though he knew it meant removing any possibility of having me for a mate.

"For another thing," he continued, ignoring what I'd said, "Imogen *would* care. She'd never allow me to defect. If she let me get away with it, others would try it too."

"So you know guys who do want to leave the Bloodbound?"

"Some. There's a good bit of grumbling about the celibacy rule—or near-celibacy," he corrected himself. "Some of the guys joined when they were very young or desperate for a reprieve from their human lives, and now they wish they could take a mate. They like being soldiers and protectors of our people but not that particular vow."

I nodded. "I would imagine it's a... challenge for young guys to live under a restriction like that."

"To say the least," he muttered.

Reece sounded like he commiserated. Remembering how passionately he'd kissed me and held me, I ventured a comment that had the potential to slam the door on our open discourse. It was too important to leave unsaid, though.

"You weren't meant to be without a mate. You're a romantic at heart. You have so much love to give, Reece."

Aaaand there was the slamming door, in the form of a frown overtaking his face.

"Not anymore. I'm not that nice, fun-loving kid you met the night of the bonfire. I've changed."

"Really? Because at times tonight you've seemed so much like that guy, I almost searched the sky for a crimson moon."

"Believe me, Abbi... I've changed."

10

NOT AN ISSUE

Reece

If Abbi knew about the real purpose of my mission, she would never have compared me to the nice small-town guy she'd met that long-ago night.

And if she knew all this wit and charm I'd been trotting out was for the sole purpose of making her fall for me again so I could dump her, she'd probably jump out of the moving car and run down the highway in the opposite direction.

I hoped she wouldn't though—figure me out, I mean. Not yet. There was an unexpected side effect to all this flirting—I was actually having a good time for the first time in about, oh, a year.

Talking to Abbi was fun, interesting in a way talking with my Bloodbound brothers was not. Not that they weren't interesting, but this was... different. Abbi was so unpredictable. Her brain worked in a completely different way from mine, and she was just so *real*, so unafraid to admit what she thought and felt, to show her true self. I liked her—maybe even more than before.

Which was *not* going to be a problem because I wasn't

going to let it be. I was going to stay in control of this thing and master my own feelings, making sure no inconvenient ones slipped through.

Only once had my control failed me, when she'd hinted that something had happened between her and Shane during their trip to the Bastion. I already knew they'd kissed, thanks to his big mouth.

What I kept wondering—what would drive me crazy if I didn't *stop* wondering—was what else might have happened.

Instead of focusing on that or listening to any more of Abbi's glowing accolades of the woman I'd been sent to assassinate, I changed the subject.

"So... where'd you get that outfit?"

For the sake of anonymity, she wore heavy eye makeup and lipstick and some *very* un-Abbi-like clothes. A pair of jeans that rode dangerously low on her hips and a charcoal gray knit top that had a metallic sheen to it.

If you just looked at the upper half of it, you'd call the top modest—the long sleeves went to her wrists, and the crew-neckline didn't reveal so much as a collarbone.

But I *wasn't* looking at the top half. I couldn't keep my eyes off the lower half, which was... not there.

The shirt, sweater, whatever the hell it was, was cropped just under her breasts with a shiny silver elastic band of fabric holding it tight around her upper rib cage.

Below that was bare skin all the way down to the dropped waistband of her jeans. That expanse of uncovered skin drew my eye like a magnet anytime I dared to glance her direction, though until now, she'd seemed completely unaware of its effect on me.

In response to my question, Abbi wrapped both arms around her midsection, giving me at least a moment of blessed relief from temptation.

"Oh, this?" She laughed in an embarrassed way. "These were in that suitcase Heather dropped off for me."

Her friend had stopped by and left the bag while Abbi was sleeping. Obviously, she'd been concerned about her friend and wanted to help. Or she'd wanted to help drive me *insane*.

"The jeans are hers, but the top belongs to my friend Larkin. We had to borrow some of her clothes after we escaped from the Safety Center so we could get out of San Francisco without being recognized. Actually, most of the things Heather put in my bag were Larkin's."

She paused and added in a near-whisper, "Unfortunately."

"Your friend Larkin has... interesting taste," I remarked dryly.

"Well, she works at Fangers—it's a theme restaurant—lots of scantily clad vampire girls serving burgers 'with bite.'"

I chuckled. "Yeah, I know what it is."

"Okay, yeah. So she has a bunch of, you know, sexy clothes for work. She pulls it off a whole lot better than I do," Abbi said, blushing a pretty pink.

"Oh, I don't know about that," I drawled. "It looks *good* on you. A little too good."

More blood rushed to her cheeks, which sent my blood rushing in a completely opposite direction.

A steady pulse started in my neck as well, and my body temperature rose a few degrees. Which was bad. I'd said it to get a rise out of *her*, not myself.

It was true, though. Yes, I'd been shamelessly flirting, but I'd also been stating an absolute fact. She looked too good for *my* good. Especially if I was going to keep the upper hand in this fake relationship of ours.

"I'm sorry," Abbi said, sounding breathless. "I didn't mean to cause you a... problem. Maybe we can stop at a store somewhere and I can buy some other—"

I reached over and covered her hand with mine. "Don't worry about it. I was just teasing you. I can handle it."

As long as I gouge my own eyes out and don't regenerate them.

"Your clothes are fine. Really."

She nodded and gave me a grateful smile. "Okay. Good. Because this is actually the *least* skimpy thing Heather packed for me."

God help me, I'm screwed.

I assured her once again the clothes were not an issue. Unfortunately, they became one when we stopped for gas again.

It was actually our last stop of the night. An hour before dawn I pulled off at an exit with signs for a gas station and vampire-friendly hotel. I planned to fill up the car then head for the hotel next door where we'd spend the daylight hours.

Instead of staying in the car this time, Abbi insisted on getting out.

"I need to stretch my legs. We've been going how long?"

I checked my watch. "Seven hours. We're on the outskirts of Buffalo."

"You must be so tired of driving." She walked toward the gas station doors and stretched her arms over her head, letting out a yawn. "I know I'm sick of sitting."

Honestly, I was tired—or I *had* been until she'd done that stretch.

Now I was wide awake, every cell in my body springing to full attention at the sight of her lean waist and flat stomach and the way her svelte back arched, drawing my eye down to the even more enticing curve of her bottom in those tight jeans.

Damn you Larkin, wherever you are.

And damn Heather for stacking the deck against me with her packing. Had she done it on purpose? Surely she hadn't believed I wouldn't *notice* Abbi's enticing figure in this attire.

Loud male voices let me know I wasn't the only one who'd noticed.

"Hey beautiful," one of them called out, slurring the words.

A group of young men—they looked like frat boys who'd pulled an all-nighter—were exiting the gas station store with bags of chips and cases of beer.

From the smell and sound of things, these were the *replacement* provisions. I had no doubt mass quantities of alcohol had already been consumed tonight.

There was a college campus at this exit, according to the last billboard I'd seen. Hopefully these guys would manage to make it back there without wiping out any fellow motorists or unfortunate pedestrians.

And for their sake, I hoped they did no more than notice Abbi and make drunken comments on her beauty. *That* I could put up with, and who could blame them?

But their inebriation—or their idiocy—made them take it further. As a group, they turned and followed her, going back into the store.

"Wait for us, honey," one of them said.

"She's hot," another said. "I think she's a vamp chick."

11

CHECKING IN

Reece

Damn it. Yanking the nozzle from my gas tank, I slammed it back onto the pump and raced after them, not bothering to even close the gas tank cover or lock my car.

When I got inside the store, the guys were already surrounding Abbi like a swarm of drones around a queen bee during mating season.

"Hey sexy," one of them said. "You don't go to U.B., do you? I'd remember seeing *you.*"

Again, it wasn't entirely their fault. Abbi was beautiful, and she *did* possess the irresistible pheromones of a queen.

The problem was, she wasn't *their* queen. She wouldn't be their victim either, not while I was anywhere close.

Abbi, who looked extremely nervous, was actually trying to answer the guy's inane question. "No, I'm not... I don't..."

"She's too sexy for college. Aren't you, honey?" his friend said.

This one made the mistake of touching her. Sliding his hand around her bare waist, he pulled her back against him and buried his about-to-be-flattened face in her hair.

Abbi was already doing a fine job of extricating herself, but even if they'd all said a polite, "I'm sorry," and walked away, it was too late. My temper was a blazing firestorm looking for something to consume.

"Get your hands off her," I ordered in my best Bloodbound commander voice.

Naturally, I wasn't wearing the uniform since we were trying to fly under the radar, but my height alone intimidated most men, and it held true in this situation.

The hair-sniffer must have been drunker than the rest because he didn't step away like the others.

"Shit, that's a huge vamp," one of his friends whispered. "Jared—dude—get away from her."

Sadly for Jared, he wasn't listening. Apparently beer-goggles didn't just make people more attractive, they must also have made them look smaller.

Instead of letting Abbi go, he gave me a smug look and reached for her again, draping an arm over her shoulders and dragging her toward his sweat-stained armpit. "She likes me, man, and I saw her first. You don't own her."

She squirmed and darted a nervous glance toward the clerk and then the store's security cameras, obviously reluctant to break the guy's arm in their view.

I didn't feel any such inhibitions.

Using my full vampire speed, I plucked his arm from her neck and jerked it up behind his back. If Abbi hadn't been watching, it might have ended up *in* his backside, but I trusted the loud crack of splintering bone made the point just as well.

"Maybe not," I whispered in his ear. "But she's still *mine*."

It was unlikely he or anyone else actually heard the words. His yowling drowned them out.

Good "friends" that they were, his companions left him

behind and scrambled for the parking lot. I escorted Jared out to them, leaving the shell-shocked group with a parting shot of The Pull.

"Have a good evening, *gentlemen*, and forget everything that happened here. Your buddy Jared picked a bar fight tonight with the wrong gang member. You should probably let the soberest among you drive him to the hospital so they can reset that arm."

Then I went back into the store and used The Pull on the cashier. "You won't remember us being here, and you'll erase the last hour of surveillance tape after we leave."

The middle-aged woman stared at me dully and said, "Yes."

Putting a supportive arm around Abbi's trembling form, I walked her to my car. I opened the passenger side door, waited for her to tuck her legs in, then closed it. Only then did I let out a shuddering breath and take a deep, calming one.

Again, I breathed in and out, willing my adrenaline level to recede and giving my own limbs the chance to stop shaking.

When I felt almost normal, I got in behind the wheel. "You okay?"

Abbi nodded rapidly several times. Her feet were pulled up onto the seat, her arms wrapped around her knees.

"I'm going to find a hotel at a different exit," I told her. "Just in case. You hang tight—you'll be in a hot shower and a soft bed before you know it."

After a few minutes of driving, her soft voice broke the silence. "You haven't changed that much, you know. You're still looking out for me."

Then she slid her hand over to cover mine on the steering wheel and rested her head against my shoulder. "Thank you."

Shit. A hotel room alone with her was the very last place I needed to be right now.

Unfortunately, the sun didn't care about the emotions currently swirling around my heart *or* what was happening below the belt. It was rising, and we had to get off the road and inside.

I pulled off at the next exit and drove to the nearest hotel. Parking close to the door, I grabbed Abbi's bag, and we walked hand-in-hand to the check-in counter to book one of its blackout rooms. They were specially designed for vampires with no external windows and a mini-fridge for blood bags.

Please let them have a double room available. Please please please.

I was strong, but I wasn't blind, deaf, and lacking a sense of smell. Plus, battle tended to get all the juices flowing, if you know what I mean. My warrior instincts didn't know the difference between a bunch of drunken frat boys and a real threat, and I was still keyed up in every way.

In other words, a single bed was *not* going to work tonight.

We couldn't take separate rooms because our cover story was that of a loving couple on vacation.

Besides, Imogen's blood *had* altered Abbi's appearance somewhat, but not *that* much. If you were really looking, which the federal authorities were, you could tell she was the same young female vampire who'd escaped the Merced Safety Center during an unexpected attack on the gates and mass exodus of inmates. She'd draw far more scrutiny traveling alone than as part of a "couple."

She wore a ballcap that covered the top of her face and took a seat on a bench in the lobby while I did all the talking at the counter.

The clerk was very friendly, especially for someone who'd been up all night. "Hello folks. Checking in?"

"Yes. We don't have a reservation," I told her, "but we've been driving all night and really need to get off the road. Do you have a double room available?"

Glancing first at my eyes then down at her computer screen, she said, "Let me look."

She tapped a few keys and looked up again, smiling. "I have one vampire room left. Looks like it's a king. Will that do?"

I blew out a quiet whistle. "Actually, could you check availability on your other rooms? Maybe we could just draw the curtains tightly?"

When she gave me a quizzical *you-don't-want-to-sleep-with-your-hot-girlfriend?* look, I hooked a thumb over my shoulder at Abbi.

"She snores."

The clerk grinned and wrinkled her nose in amusement. "Okay, lemme see what I've got."

Frowning at the screen a minute later, she said, "I'm sorry, sir, but it looks like all we have left are rooms on the east side of the building with exterior windows. Even with the curtains drawn, I'm afraid there's a chance of some daylight sneaking in. I'd hate for anybody to get burned."

"I understand," I said.

Reaching for the phone she said, "I can call some of the other hotels at this exit for you and see if they have any doubles available."

She really was a nice girl. I reached for my wallet. "No, that's okay. We'd have to get back in the car and drive there, and the sun's up already. We'll take the king room. It'll be fine."

She smiled at me and processed the payment then handed

me a key along with directions to the elevator. We thanked her and turned to go, but she called me back.

"Sir?"

"Yes?"

The clerk held out a small packet wrapped in plastic. "Maybe these will help? Earplugs."

"Ah." I smiled at her and took the offering, though of course my *ears* weren't the problem.

1 2

STILL AWAKE

Reece

As far as I knew, neither of us snored.

On the other hand, maybe Abbi *did* snore. I'd never slept with her—slept *in the same room* with her, I mentally corrected myself.

Too late. Parts of my anatomy that had taken a back seat for the confrontation with the beer buzz squad were once again awake and jostling for a spot at the front of the line.

"Thanks a lot. I'll be sure to write you a great review," I told the young woman behind the counter.

She beamed at me. "Thank you so much. That would be awesome."

As we rode up in the elevator, Abbi yawned again. "I think I'm finally calming down. In fact, I feel exhausted now."

"Conflict will do that to you. I'm usually wired for hours after any kind of situation, but then when I come down, I *really* crash."

"Thank you again. I wasn't sure what to do back there, you know? Nothing like that has ever happened to me. I mean, some of the guards in the Safety Center were kind of creepy, but you could usually avoid them, and they knew there were cameras everywhere."

My aggression, which had just now started to dial down, kicked in again.

"There was this one guy, Gatlin." She was quiet for a moment before saying, "He got what was coming to him."

"Good."

We got off the elevator on the third floor and stopped in front of a door on the interior side of the hall.

"Is this us, 335?" she asked.

"Home sweet home," I said before thinking then cringed as I swiped the key card. We were not an actual couple, and this was not our cozy little abode.

Abbi didn't seem to notice the faux pas. She stepped into the room and flicked on the lights. When she got past the entry area, though, she stopped cold.

"There's only one... bed."

Moving past her, I placed our bags on a low wood laminate table. I did my best to make my tone unconcerned. "Yep. It's all they had."

"They had no rooms with two beds?" Abbi asked in a small voice.

"They did not. Not interior rooms anyway. Besides, this is better for safety's sake. At least it's a king," I added with exaggerated cheerfulness.

Her joints seemed to unhinge, and she stepped farther into the sleeping area. "Yeah. That's true. It's pretty big."

"Huge," I said then cringed again. I unzipped my duffle bag and rummaged around in it, just to have something to do. Finding our blood bag supply and the ice packs, I put them in the mini-fridge.

After another minute of silently staring at the bed, Abbi went to her bag and pulled out a travel toothbrush, toothpaste, and makeup remover. She also grabbed an oversized t-shirt and a pair of panties she balled up in her hand in an attempt to hide them from me.

As if it was a secret she wore panties. Red panties that appeared to be quite small and made of some sort of lacy fabric. *Oh God.*

"Mind if I use the bathroom first?" she asked. "I think I might take a shower. I know all I did was sit in the car today, but after that guy touched me..."

"By all means. Take your time."

Of course she was grossed out after what she'd been through. It made me feel even worse about the thoughts that had been running through my head.

I may or may not have been fantasizing about accidentally-on-purpose rolling over to her side of the bed during my "sleep." In that fantasy, the t-shirt had ridden up and exposed the red—

No. Just stop it. You're torturing yourself and getting the whole make her fall in love *plan ass-backwards.*

Again.

Abbi wasn't even trying, and she was twisting me into knots of frustrated desire. *I* was supposed to be seducing *her.*

Not tonight though. Not after what she'd been through at the gas station. Unlike that drunk idiot, I'd be keeping my hands and all other appendages firmly on my side of the bed. No matter what she had on under that t-shirt.

It promised to be more challenging than the most grueling of the Bloodbound recruit trials. Abbi emerged from the steamy bathroom, her hair and face shiny clean and the rest of her smelling so sweet and alluring I almost excused myself to go swim some laps in the hotel's indoor pool.

Now her mid-section was covered, and it was her legs that were exposed to my hungry eyes. Long and curvy and silky smooth, they would feel incredible tangled with mine under the sheets.

"Your turn," she said sweetly.

"Right. Thanks."

My shower was ice cold. On purpose. And I made it extra-long. Maybe by the time I finished and was frozen solid, she'd be asleep.

When I got out, I realized I'd neglected to bring anything that could reasonably be considered sleepwear. I wasn't used to sleeping in co-ed company, and I always went to bed in just my boxers.

Well, I'd make sure to slip into bed quietly and avoid waking her. Then I'd wake early and get dressed before she woke up.

Abbi looked so small in the large bed. She was still and quiet, and I slid under the sheets, grateful my desperate prayers had been answered.

But after a minute of lying there drinking in the scent of her skin and listening to her soft breaths, I realized she was still awake.

13

WITH A WHISPER

Reece

She rolled over to face me in the dark. "Reece?"

My brain and body jolted into full alert mode. "Yeah?"

"I've never slept in the same bed with a guy before."

And now my brain and body were high-fiving each other. That answered the question about Shane. He may have kissed her, but he hadn't gotten any further. Maybe I'd let him live.

"I mean, I slept with Shane in the back of a big rig..."

Nope. He was a dead man.

"... but Kelly and Heather were there too, and we just... slept. And he was in handcuffs."

And once again, Shane had a future.

This girl was giving me whiplash. I'd never experienced higher highs and lower lows than I felt when I was with her.

"Are you saying you'd like me to wear handcuffs?" I joked.

She giggled, a lovely sound that sent waves of joy rolling through my chest and then downward.

"No silly. I trust you," she said. "I was just wondering... have you slept with many girls?"

At my extended silence, she quickly added, "I mean, I know you don't sleep with anyone but Imogen now, but..."

After another long hesitation, I corrected her wrong assumption. "I haven't slept with Imogen."

Abruptly she pushed up to one elbow. Her long hair hung down, nearly covering half her face. The eye I could see was wide with shock.

"You haven't?"

"No. She's never summoned me to her chambers for that reason."

Was it my imagination or had Abbi just let out a long sigh? That was when I realized she was jealous of Imogen. Not because of her unique beauty or her immense power.

Because of me.

Suddenly I was breathing like I'd just come off a thirty-mile training run. Abbi's breathing had become audible, too. She was nervous. Or excited. Or both. Whatever it was, the palpable energy she was giving off was doing terrible things to me.

Her next question was so timid and breathy I almost didn't hear it. "Are you... disappointed?"

"Disappointed?" Why on earth would she think I'd be disappointed about not sleeping with a two-hundred-year old woman?

"Yeah. You know, because she's the only woman you can..." Her shyness prevented her from finishing.

I glanced around the dark, empty room, which was ridiculous. It wasn't like we'd been followed, and we'd picked a hotel at random. There were no listening devices in here. But I was about to make a risky confession.

"No. I'm not disappointed. I never wanted her that way."

"Oh." A long pause. "And other girls?"

"There were no other girls."

"Really?" I could tell she didn't believe me.

"Really. I was a classic late bloomer in high school. Even if a girl had been interested in me, I wouldn't have noticed it—or had any idea what to do about it."

"And college?"

"I was in the middle of first semester freshman year when I met you at that bonfire. I dated some, but I lived in the athletic dorm with my teammates. We weren't allowed to have girls in our rooms. And I guess I never went out with a girl who liked me enough to invite me back to her room."

"I seriously doubt that." Abbi's tone was much lower than her usual speaking voice. The sound of it curled around my belly and made me feel like that awkward college freshman again.

"Well, they weren't allowed to have guys in their dorm rooms either," I said. "Maybe if I'd gone out with an upperclassman who lived off-campus, I would've gotten lucky."

"Maybe," she said, and we both laughed.

Abbi got serious again. "But I'm glad you didn't."

A flush moved through my body, raising its temperature by several degrees.

This was dangerous. Abigail Byler and Reece Hendrix had zero business discussing the topic of sex. Especially lying in bed together face to face. And yet I couldn't seem to stop myself from probing further.

"And you... I guess your community standards sort of prevented pre-marital sex?"

"Not sort of. Completely. No opportunity. No one I was interested in that way, anyway."

"So then..." *Don't ask, Reece. Do. Not. Ask.* "Did you *ever* meet anyone you *were* interested in... that way?"

My heartbeat pounded so hard in my ears I was worried she could hear it too. She probably could, in fact.

Her eyes answered my question before her words did.

"I think you know the answer to that."

And that was how my "master plan" to seduce Abbi and break her heart died—with a whisper.

Or maybe it had crashed and burned back at the gas station when she'd been threatened by those guys and needed my help.

How had I ever thought I could hurt this girl?

All I wanted to do was *protect* her from harm. Well, okay, that wasn't *all* I wanted to do, but it was the extent of what I would allow myself to do.

And how had I ever believed I could get this close to her and spend this much time with her without falling head over heels back in love? Maybe I'd never stopped loving her.

Either way, I was screwed.

I couldn't help how I felt, but I *could* stop this from going any further. We hadn't done anything to earn Imogen's death penalty—yet.

All I had to do was break this unbelievable soul-penetrating eye contact... and stop our breaths from mingling... and definitely stop myself from moving toward her mouth...

Abbi placed a small hand on my chest and stretched toward me, bringing her lips within millimeters of mine. My heart beat so hard and so fast it was literally painful.

Clenching every muscle in my body, I fought the overwhelming urge to close that miniscule distance and kiss her, wrap my arms around her, and pull her against me, under me—okay this wasn't working.

I have to move away from her.

It took every ounce of strength I possessed, but I managed to roll over, turning to face the other wall and drawing deep, controlled breaths.

"Good night, Abbi," I gritted out.

This time I was sure I heard a sigh. "Sleep well, Reece."

14

HAIL KING PARKER

Abbi

I wasn't sure if Reece slept well, but I did not.

Not only did his massive size take up a ridiculous amount of the king mattress, his legs and arms kept wandering into my relatively small sliver of space. Every time I'd manage to calm myself enough to drift off, some part of him would touch some part of me, and I'd snap back awake again.

He *seemed* to be sleeping pretty soundly. Maybe it was that thing he'd mentioned about a post-battle let down. Perhaps the adrenaline crash explained why he'd rolled away and started snoring instead of accepting my pathetically obvious invitation to kiss me.

Or maybe he likes his head attached *to his neck, dodo.*

Right. The Bloodbound vows. Reece might not have slept with Imogen—*yay yippee and yahooooo!!!*—but he was still loyal to her.

Not so *yay*. But reality rarely was.

The reality this evening was that we still had about six hours left to go to Sudbury. Unless we wanted to play another game of Russian roulette in another hotel room at dawn—not smart—we needed to pack up and get on the road.

I woke Reece then dressed and gathered my things as quickly as I could. To save time, we opted to bring our blood bags along and drink them in the car rather than enjoy them in the room.

Actually, I didn't know anyone who *enjoyed* blood bags. There was just nothing yummy about the taste of cold blood. It was sustenance rather than satisfaction. The alternative was monstrous, though.

"Did you ever drink blood from the vein?" I asked Reece.

"What?" He whipped his head toward me, sounding like he'd been pulled from deep thought.

"Blood. From a person instead of a blood bag."

His face, which had worn an almost dreamy expression before, turned sour. "Yes. Did you?"

"Yes. Just that once with Josiah. Since then I've stuck to the blood bags. Have you done it since you came to the Bastion?"

"Are you asking me if Imogen made me take the test?"

"I wasn't exactly, but now that you brought it up... did she?"

He shook his head. "She's not interested in whether I've got 'the gift.' I guess it has no value in the Crimson Court if you're male."

"Consider yourself lucky on that count. So then, when you're out with the Bloodbound you never..."

"No. Why do you ask?"

"Well, when Kannon and his team rescued me at that border checkpoint, some of the guys, um... finished off the police officer and the border agent. I guess they decided not to let all that blood go to waste. I just wondered if sometimes on the job you drank from humans."

"No," he said in a definitive way. "I've had relatively little interaction with humans since becoming Bloodbound. My work has consisted mostly of tracking and bringing in rogues. Since Imogen made me captain of her queensguard, I rarely get out to do even that. I've been supervising my men, training new queensguard recruits, stuff like that."

Shifting in his seat, he added, "And my experiences when I first turned left me with, shall we say, a bad taste in my mouth about drinking from humans."

"You never did tell me what you remembered about those days once your mind cleared from the animal blood."

Reece shifted again, his mouth forming a hard, unwilling line. "I don't really like to talk about it."

The night I'd left him behind at the Bastion, Reece had said some things to me I'd never forgotten. One was that he *deserved* to spend eternity enslaved to Imogen because of something he'd done. I disagreed then, and I felt even more strongly about it now.

Maybe if he'd just *tell* me what he'd done, I could convince him he was wrong, that what he deserved, like all of us, was forgiveness and a fresh start.

"I told you about biting Josiah," I prompted.

Reece rolled his lower lip in then out, exhaling loudly. "Yes. I did drink human blood right after turning. I attacked my family."

"Oh. Did you k—did they die?"

"No. I stopped before draining them completely, but I... hurt them. And I didn't stop there. I went on a sort of rampage. I bit a *lot* of people."

My next question was hushed. "Did they turn?"

He was quiet for so long I thought he wasn't going to answer. But then he did. "Yes. *All* of them."

For a few moments there was only the sound of the tires on the road and the soft patter of rain on the windshield. Reece had inherited Imogen's "gift." He could turn a human with a single bite, and he'd turned his whole family.

I touched his arm. "I'm so sorry."

He nodded but didn't look at me, just kept going in a monotone voice. "I can never go home again—or anywhere near there. My family hates me. I basically terrorized my hometown, leaving brand new vampires in my wake. I'm the worst kind of rogue. I should have been destroyed."

My fingers on his arm tightened, and I leaned down, craning my neck to the side to look at his face, to try to get *him* to look at *me*.

"No—you shouldn't have. It wasn't your fault. You didn't know what you were doing. The only reason I didn't do the same thing is that Kannon found me early on and brought me in. Is that why you started drinking animal blood? The guilt?"

He nodded. "I was really shaken by what I'd done. I was determined to resist drinking from humans, but the thirst was so powerful. I hoped the animal blood would satisfy me. Unfortunately, it turned me into a freaking psycho."

"Look, Reece... I don't mean to be insensitive, but in the grand scheme of things what you did was not that bad."

"Not that bad? I just told you I *turned* my parents and my brothers and God only knows how many other people."

"Yes. I get it, and that *is* bad—if they had no interest in becoming vampires. You changed their lives forever, but you didn't *take* their lives. It's not bad enough for you to think you don't deserve freedom and the right to still live your own life."

"If you're going to try to convince me again to defect from the Bloodbound—"

"I'm just saying I don't understand why you didn't think you could tell me about this before. What you did is no worse than what I did to Josiah and his family."

Reece's scowl melted into a blank expression, and he stared straight ahead out the windshield where the rain had begun to fall harder.

"I don't want to talk about this anymore. The subject is closed, okay?"

Heaving a heavy sigh, I said, "Okay."

Suddenly noticing it was cold in the car, I cranked the heat up to knock off the chill.

The sky looked strange, a bank of thick nimbostratus clouds hanging low overhead and giving it the appearance of dusk, though it was much later.

Precipitation continued to strike the windshield with a light tapping noise. It didn't sound like rain, though, now that I was paying attention. It sounded icy.

Well, we *were* on our way to Canada. What were the chances of making it all the way there without any weather issues?

"Is it supposed to snow today?" I asked. *Might as well talk about the weather since we can't talk about anything important.*

Reece bent to view a larger picture of the sky through the windshield. "I guess it snows every day somewhere in December. We're passing through so many states, odds are we'll get hit with it eventually, especially since we're going north."

"We should check the forecast. Snow or freezing rain would really slow us down."

I turned on news radio, hoping to hear a local weather report.

Reece chuckled. "Your Amish roots are showing."

He opened the car's center console and pulled out a phone, offering it to me. "Try this."

"Oh, right." I searched national radar, locating a small system moving through this area and the possibility of a larger one up ahead. We'd have to keep an eye on it.

We left the radio on and listened for a while. Working for Sadie, I'd gotten used to keeping up with current events—especially those that had a direct impact on the vampire community.

After a few minutes, the host threw the coverage to a live report from President Parker's latest rally.

Though he wouldn't be running for re-election for almost four years, he continued to hold big events where he whipped his audience into a near-frenzy of adoration for him and hatred of anyone who wasn't exactly like them—vampires in particular.

Having met with him a few times, Sadie speculated that Parker didn't necessarily even believe in what he was saying—he just craved the slobbering idolization of his supporters and would say anything they wanted to hear in order to get the ego boost from their worship.

In that way, he wasn't much different from Imogen.

I reached for the dial, intending to change the station. I'd heard enough already to know this speech wouldn't be any different from the rest of them.

Reece held up a hand. "Wait. I want to listen for a minute. It's good to take the temperature of things in the outside world every so often."

"... and we're gonna drive 'em out of our neighborhoods," the president was saying.

There were loud cheers. "And we're gonna drive 'em out of our schools."

More cheers. "And we're gonna drive them out of the workforce and give jobs back to hard-working, God-fearing Americans who stayed on the straight and narrow instead of choosing the path of darkness."

Tremendous cheers and shouts of "Hail King Parker," and "Stake the vamps! Save the humans!" blared through the radio.

I gritted my teeth and squeezed my eyelids shut, trying desperately to employ my Amish community's policy of praying for our enemies instead of hating them.

It wasn't easy. What about those of us who hadn't chosen to become vampires? Like me, and Reece, and Kelly, and Larkin, and—well, I knew of too many others to name them all. A lot of us *were* God-fearing Americans and didn't want anything to do with 'darkness'—except for of course the fact we had to live our lives at night.

"We're gonna drive them *out* of this country and *back* to the mouth of Hell from whence they came," Parker continued. "But I need your help. Donations to my—"

Reece reached up and snapped the radio off in a furious motion. "Sorry I made you listen to that."

"No, you're right. It's important to be aware of what's going on."

"Like we can *avoid* being aware of it. How many billboards for hotels and restaurants have we seen on this trip that said 'no vamps' in bold letters? Things are getting worse, not better."

His grip on the steering wheel tightened until his fists shook, and he let out an angry sound.

"It makes me so mad. *This* is why we need the Bloodbound. We *have* to fight back."

15

ANY OTHER REASON

Abbi

I hadn't seen Reece this irate since he'd first been brought into the med clinic at the Bastion.

It was hard to blame him, but still I felt the need to talk him down from his enraged state.

"There are other ways of fighting, you know. Sadie's media appearances and peaceful protests were making some headway with public opinion. And the VHC employed a whole team of lawyers who fought unfair policies in the courts."

Reece rolled his eyes. "Yeah, I was gonna be one of those someday—before I was turned and my college career ended."

"You wanted to be a lawyer? I would have thought you hoped to play professional basketball."

"Nah. I mean, sure, that could have been fun, but players like me were a dime a dozen. I'm tall, but I was nothing special."

He gave a sad laugh. "Now I could run circles around the other players and dunk with one finger. Of course, vampires aren't allowed in the NBA—or college hoops."

78

"I think you would have made a great lawyer," I said, once again trying to distract him from the unfairness of it all. "You're incredibly smart, and you're a voracious reader. You're also very persuasive when you want to be."

He slid a glance at me, and the edges of his mouth turned up in a reluctant smile.

"Also, you're really good at arguing," I teased.

Reece's smile grew. "I *was* the president of the debate team in high school."

"That doesn't surprise me one bit."

I studied his profile, so strong and handsome—even more so when he smiled like this. God, I loved looking at him. If he *were* to become a lawyer, there wasn't a jury on the planet that wouldn't side with him every time.

"You know, with all those skills, you didn't *really* need me to come along and help you talk to Sadie," I said.

Reece's smile dropped, and he sat straighter in his seat. "I wasn't sure she'd even speak to me without a go-between."

"She would have. She's willing to listen to anyone who has something valuable to say. And an offer of cooperation with the Crimson Court is valuable."

The icy precipitation increased, and Reece seemed to want to focus on the road, which was smart. I stopped talking so he could concentrate.

Unfortunately, the rain and sleet turned into heavy snowfall. The highway department's salt trucks couldn't manage to keep up with it. The road conditions steadily worsened until the Charger's tires were sliding more often than they rolled.

We weren't the only ones having trouble. The farther we went, the more cars we saw in the median or off on the shoulder.

When the wind picked up, turning the snowstorm into

whiteout conditions, Reece put on his turn signal and started making his way to the right lane.

"We're gonna have to get off the road for the day, let this storm pass. We're only a few hours away, but it's too hazardous to keep going in this."

"Okay."

Though it would mean another stay in a hotel room, he was probably right. A collision could result in a car fire or even one of us being decapitated, both of which were deadly to vampires.

At the very least, a car accident could leave us without a working vehicle, and public transportation was out of the question.

This time the hotel room we checked into did have two beds. Which was a good thing. Really.

So why did I feel a sinking sense of disappointment when the clerk had cheerfully announced he could accommodate Reece's request?

Don't be stupid, Abbi. Mind on the mission, remember?

As we unpacked and got ready for bed, my mind was actually on something else—our conversation from earlier about Reece's excellent persuasive skills and the fact he'd interceded with Imogen and asked to bring me along on his mission.

The truth was, he *didn't* need me to help him obtain an audience with Sadie—especially now that the VHC had been attacked and she was more likely than ever to want to connect with potential allies. He had to realize that.

Which left only one explanation for why Reece had stuck his neck out for me. He'd wanted to protect me from Imogen. He'd wanted me with *him*.

I sat on the edge of my bed, watching him move around the room. He'd brushed his teeth and showered, but he'd put his clothes back on instead of emerging from the bathroom in only his boxers as he had last night.

Too bad. I couldn't touch but looking never hurt anyone, did it?

When he'd put his shirt back on, he hadn't buttoned it up all the way. My eyes kept straying to the open neckline and the glimpses of chest muscle it afforded.

Wow. Was it hot in this room?

Reece glanced up, and our eyes met and held for a moment. I swore sometimes he could hear my thoughts.

"Are you about ready for bed?" he asked. "I'll turn out the light."

"Yeah. Okay," I wheezed, feeling breathless.

After another long moment of searing eye contact, Reece moved to the light switch and the room went dark.

I heard the sounds of him removing his clothing and sliding under the bed covers. Not helping the breathing at all.

He was only a few feet from me, but after last night's closeness and the tight quarters of the car for the past few days, it felt too far away. I lay there in my much-too-roomy bed and pictured him lying in his bed. In his boxers.

Apparently sleeping wasn't going to be any easier this time than it had been last time.

His voice came out of the darkness, deep and rough and absolutely toe-curling in its appeal.

"Abbi? You awake?"

"Yes."

"There *was* another reason for my request to bring you along... I mean, besides just needing an in with Sadie."

My pulse shot up to the ceiling. "There was?"

"I couldn't leave you there at her mercy. I'm not sure you fully understand how angry she was with you for leaving."

"I guess leaving her for her sister was pretty insulting," I said.

"Yes, but more than that, she was worried about you forming a rival 'hive' of vampires."

"She thought I was going to compete with her?" The idea was ludicrous.

"She talked about how powerful you were—about the strength of your allure." After a beat, he added, "She wasn't wrong."

A tingly feeling circulated through my body. During the trip, Reece had made a few provocative remarks, but he hadn't come right out and called me "alluring" before. Did he mean as a potential queen... or as a woman?

"I certainly don't feel powerful," I said honestly. "And she above all people should know I have no interest in ever becoming a queen."

"She knows you don't want it—now. But the potential is there. And then of course there's the chance you could someday produce biological offspring. If you did, that would set up a dynasty in the vampire world that could never be challenged by anyone—including her."

"Wow." My head spun with this new information. "So then, you got me out of there because you thought she was going to kill me."

"Yes."

For a few minutes, I was quiet, trying to work up the nerve to ask the real question on my mind.

"Was there any other reason?"

"What do you mean?" He huffed a quiet laugh. "Wanting to save your life isn't enough?"

"Well... I wondered if maybe... I hoped..." I had to stop and take a fortifying breath before continuing. "I hoped that maybe you also wanted to be with me, to spend time together."

"Abbi..." Reece's voice held a warning note.

I ignored it.

"Reece—I missed you. So much. The whole time I was away, I could never manage to *stop* missing you. I thought of you all the time. I kept thinking I saw you in different places around LA, even though I knew it couldn't possibly be you. I could never manage the least bit of interest in another guy because I was still so caught up in you."

"You left easily enough," he grumbled.

He thought it had been easy for me to leave? I was stunned.

"It was the hardest thing I've ever done. I didn't want to be separated from you. But I *couldn't* stay—not when you were bound to Imogen for eternity. It hurt too much to see you every day and not be with you. And seeing you with her was..."

The memories were so sickening I couldn't even finish the sentence.

"I told you I was never with her that way," he said quietly.

"I know. I know. And selfishly, I'm glad," I admitted. "But you were never going to be with me that way either—at least not for a few millennia. By that time, I would have gone mad. Being constantly close to you and yet so far removed would have killed me day by day until there was nothing left of me when our time finally came.

"I thought putting physical distance between us would help, but it didn't. Reece... I loved you too much to stay. I still love you."

Rustling from the other bed told me he was no longer lying under the sheets but sitting up. In the dimness of the room, I could see him sitting on the edge of his bed, facing me.

"You don't love me," he insisted. "You *can't*."

16
NOT EVEN YOU

Reece

My heart thrashed inside my chest, thrown into a frenzy by Abbi's sweet, terrible confession.

"You can't love me. I'm Bloodbound."

"That doesn't change how I feel," she insisted.

She'd moved to sit up, staying in her own bed, thank God, but facing me only feet away. I could literally feel her enticing warmth and passion from here.

"It was the pendant—my blood," I suggested. "I should never have given that to you."

"That did make me feel close to you—and it saved my life after I was shot—but it's not what I'm talking about. I do love you. I always have."

Inappropriate joy warred with justified shame inside me. "You wouldn't say that if you knew everything I've done. You wouldn't love me—you'd hate me."

"Are you talking about the people you bit? About turning your family?" she asked. "Reece, I already told you that doesn't matter to me. No one who understands what it's like to turn could blame you for that—me least of all."

She scooted even closer until our knees were nearly touching. "Not only did I turn Josiah, my actions resulted in him wiping out his family. So technically, I'm worse than you are."

I closed my eyes, letting out a heavy exhale. "That's not true."

"It *is*."

She came off the bed and reached for me. I stood, catching her hand in the air, preventing her from touching me or coming any closer. If she did, I'd never be able to get through this.

"No, Abbi. It's not. You're not the one to blame for those people's deaths... I am."

"What? Reece, you had nothing to do with—"

"Just shut up and listen to me, okay? Please?"

The sounds of my labored breaths mixed with her shallow ones.

"After I left my hometown, I went looking for you," I said. "I tracked you from the accident scene back to your village. Then I followed your scent to the farm."

"You were there?"

I nodded, though it was doubtful she could see me. Her hand was still in mine, but it had gone slack.

"I was desperate to find you, and I kind of hoped I wouldn't, too. I wasn't sure what would happen if I did see you again—I thought you were still human at the time," I explained.

"I still hadn't tried animal blood at that point, and my thirst never seemed to cease. It felt sort of tangled up with the last emotion I'd been feeling as a human—extreme desire —for you."

Abbi let out a quiet gasp, but she didn't speak, just let me continue damning myself.

"I went to the barn, stood there looking up. I could hear

you breathing, hear your heartbeat. I hadn't decided yet whether to go up and talk to you—I was afraid I might hurt you—and then a wagon pulled into the drive. Your friend Josiah was in it with an older couple. I ran and hid behind the house."

"That was the night they died," she said in a reverent tone.

"That's right." *And don't I know it.*

"I don't remember everything about that night, but I remember watching and listening as you climbed the tree and went into his room. And then you left. I knew from eavesdropping on your conversation you had both been turned. I could tell he wasn't going to make it in this life. Even as small and innocent as you were, you were much stronger than him. You had this... determination. I decided I would reveal myself to you when you returned from town."

"Why didn't you Reece? Why did you leave? We could have gone through this together. We could have helped each other. We could have avoided the Bastion altogether."

Squeezing her hand, I urged her to sit back on her bed. "Just let me finish. After you left, I sat on the ground against the house, listening to the whispers inside, the everyday noises of people getting ready for bed. Josiah's parents were kind, they were worried about him—and about what their friends and neighbors would think—but mostly they were worried about him. In spite of my burning throat and the aching emptiness of my stomach, I felt good listening to them, knowing there were at least some people in the world who'd try to understand and accept us."

I swallowed hard. This was the hardest part of the story to recall, much less say out loud. But Abbi needed to hear it. She needed to know.

"Then I caught the scent of blood. I don't know if the man cut himself shaving or maybe the woman slipped with a kitchen knife... that's where my memories end. I must have gone into a blood frenzy and killed them. Maybe I killed Josiah, too."

She came off the bed again and grabbed my hands. "You couldn't have. I saw his ashes the next morning. He killed himself by exposing himself to the sun. And if you were in a frenzy, how can you be sure you're the one who killed his parents?"

Removing my hands from her grasp, I clenched my gut against a swell of nausea. "Based on my previous behavior, that's what I would have done. What makes more sense? Your little upstanding Amish boyfriend getting up from his prayers, unlocking his door, and going downstairs to slaughter his parents or me smelling blood and doing what I'd already done multiple times in the days leading up to that? Besides, that's what Imogen said happened. She told me on the night of the Inception Ceremony."

It was the information that had tipped me over the edge and driven the last nail in the coffin of my humanity.

It was the information that had proven to me once and for all that Abbi was better off without me.

How could I have gone with her to Los Angeles and presented myself as one of the good guys, ready to fight for peace, justice, and the American vampire way, knowing what I'd done?

"Imogen?" Abbi said, sounding baffled. "She wasn't there. How would she know what happened?"

"She *knew*, okay? She's our maker. She laid it out for me in gory detail, described the farm, what they looked like, everything. She knew where to find you, didn't she? She sent Kannon after you."

Abbi was quiet for a minute before speaking again. "And this is what you've been hiding from me? This is the 'terrible secret' that made you feel so unworthy of love you enslaved yourself for an eternity."

"Yes. I'm the reason you lost your best friend, your community, your whole way of life."

"You're an idiot."

My head snapped back in surprise. "What?"

"You're an idiot if you really believed that would keep me from loving you."

"I murdered the people you considered your second parents. Josiah *killed* himself because of me. And you blamed yourself for it."

"None of it would have happened if I hadn't chosen to turn Josiah in the first place."

"And I caused the accident on the highway that started everything," I argued.

Abbi rose again and put a soft finger over my lips. "Even if it *was* you who killed the Yoders, and even if you *had* killed Josiah, it wouldn't change things. I'm sad about their deaths, but I had to learn this lesson for myself, and you need to learn it, too—you can't change the past. There is nothing and no one beyond forgiveness. Not even you."

I sat back on the edge of my bed, stunned. Abbi moved forward, coming to a stop just in front of me, standing between my spread knees. Before I could prevent it, she put her hands on my shoulders, then slid them up to clasp my jaw.

She looked down into my face, her eyes shining in the darkness. "I forgive you, Reece. For whatever you've done... for whatever you might do in the future. You are the most important person in the world to me, and there is nothing you could ever do that would stop me from loving you."

For long excruciating seconds I remained motionless, staring back at her, drinking in the love in her eyes and preserving every line of her beautiful face in my mind's eye so I'd never forget a single detail of this moment.

17

THE ANSWER FOR NOW

Reece

When I finally released the floodgates, it was more like a tsunami than a wave.

I literally couldn't keep the emotion inside any longer. My arms went around Abbi, pulling her down on top of me and bringing her lips to mine.

Stroking her back and hair and face, I spoke between fervent kisses, letting the words and passion I felt for her crash over her, drowning her in my love.

"God, I love you. You have no idea how much I burned for you while you were away. It was even worse when you came back. When I saw you in that corridor outside the clinic, I thought I was going to spontaneously combust."

"Me too," she said. "I was overwhelmed to see you. I didn't think I could love you more, but when I saw you again it all came rushing back, and it was like it had doubled somehow."

I kissed her again deeply, trying with my lips and tongue to express the truth behind my words. "Since then, I've been in agony, wondering how I was going to survive eternity without holding you and kissing you and making you mine, wondering how I was going to keep us both alive if Imogen suspected. I still don't know the answer to that one, but I don't care anymore. I can't hide from you anymore."

"I don't want you to. I don't want us ever to hide our feelings from each other again," she said.

For a few minutes there were no words as our mouths and hands devoured each other. Then Abbi pulled back slightly, speaking against my mouth, which wasn't nearly finished with her.

"We do have to hide it from Imogen, though."

"I would never let her hurt you," I vowed. "That's why I had to get you out of there. I'd die before letting anything happen to you."

Abbi's hands came up to bracket my face, holding it in place. "No. Reece... you can't say that. I couldn't bear it if anything happened to *you*. We have to be careful. Promise me we'll be careful."

She was so sweet and sincere and so incredibly beautiful and sexy I would have promised to pluck a star from the sky for her if she asked.

"We will. She'll never know."

I wasn't even sure what I was saying, I just wanted another taste of Abbi's delicious lips. I dived in again, holding her against my burning skin, wishing it was possible to pull her inside myself.

After a minute, she broke the kiss. "What if she knows already? What if she can... *see* us somehow?"

She was doing her best to break the *mood* with that question. After waiting so long for this moment, I wasn't having it. I kissed her again.

"She can't. Don't think about her right now."

Flipping Abbi over so I hovered above her on the bed, I started moving down her body, kissing her neck, then working down the center of her chest to her stomach.

Abbi grabbed my shoulders, stopping me. "But... you said she saw what happened at the Yoders' farm. She described the scene to you. She's not just my maker, she's yours, too. She might be watching us right now."

A shiver raised gooseflesh on her warm, smooth skin. I attempted to kiss it away, but Abbi wiggled from my grasp, rolling to the other side of my bed.

"I'm serious, Reece. Even if she can't see us now, she'll know when we get back to the Bastion. She'll be able to tell —I just know she will. You're bound to her. We can't do this."

I rolled over onto my back and covered my face with both hands, blowing out a breath of frustrated desire. "*Now* you're worried about the Bloodbound vows?"

There wasn't one part of my body that wanted to shift focus from Abbi to Imogen, but she was forcing the matter.

"You know how much I hate it, but it's still true," she said. "You said you'd die before letting her hurt me? I feel the same way about you. I can't be a part of something that'll get you killed."

Making one last attempt, I rolled up onto my shoulder to face her and dragged her close to me again. "For me, it would be *worth* it. If I could have one night with you, I'd die a happy man."

Abbi's expression melted but then she put a small palm against my chest, holding me back from renewing our impassioned activities.

"Don't say that. I don't want just one night with you—I want eternity," she said. "We can't have that. Not yet. Not without Sadie's help. We have to keep our heads on straight and focus on getting to her. This mission has to succeed, or it won't be just us who suffers—it'll be the whole world."

At her mention of "our" mission, the last of my ramped-up excitement subsided. "So what are you suggesting? That I take back everything I just said, and we go back to being 'friends?'"

She ran her gaze over me, taking in my naked torso and arms, my shoulders, my mouth. "I don't think *that* is possible. I could never be just friends with you. But I think... for now... it would be best if we avoided situations like... this."

"Can I still kiss you?"

A tortured look of pained temptation crossed her face. "I don't think that would be wise."

Abbi's lush body was still pressed against mine, her soft breasts cushioning my chest, the sleep t-shirt bunched somewhere around her waist, leaving her smooth legs free to tangle with mine.

Her rapid breaths tickled my hungry lips, and from the pace of her heartbeat, I surmised it was just as hard for her to resist crushing them to mine as it was for me to keep my mouth off of her.

If I hadn't been bathed in sexual frustration, I might have laughed at the absurdity of it all.

My hand coasted from her back downward, sliding over her curves and pulling her lower body more tightly against mine.

"What about this?" I whispered against her lips, not kissing her but not *not*-kissing her either. "Can I do this? Would this be wise?"

Abbi let out a shuddering breath. "Reece..."

Her breathy plea did nothing to discourage me. My excitement kicked into high gear again. Instead of kissing her mouth, which she'd instructed me not to do, I dropped my lips to her neck, nuzzling the warm, intoxicating skin before opening my mouth to taste it.

For a moment, she allowed it, groaning in pleasure and squirming against me in a maddening rhythm.

Then those little hands worked their way between us

again, and she pushed herself back. With great difficulty, apparently. "We can't. I have to get out of this bed. You feel too good. You make *me* feel too good."

"I want to Abbi," I nearly begged. "I've never wanted anything so much in my life. Let me make you feel good."

With another groan—this one not quite so happy as the last—she kicked her legs and scrambled backward, popping out of the bed on the other side.

"You're impossible to say no to. But you're asking me to sign your death sentence. And I *have* to find the strength to say no to that."

Walking quickly back to her own bed, she got in and pulled the covers up to her chin.

"So in regard to your question about kissing—and all the other stuff—the answer—for now—is no."

18

A PLAN I COULD GET BEHIND

Abbi

Looking over at Reece's astonished face, I saw the moment sexual excitement converted to frustration.

"So it's okay for you to kiss *Shane* but not me," he said in a bitter voice.

"This has nothing to do with him. This is about you and me."

"You're damn right it is. But every time I think about him putting his mouth on you, I want to punch a wall. Or the dashboard—or whatever inanimate surface is handy."

"It only happened once," I began.

"*Twice*. He kissed you in the clinic—I was there, remember?"

"Yes. Clearly. You made your presence—and your disapproval—obvious to everyone involved. As I was saying, it only happened *twice,* and it won't be happening again. I don't feel that way about Shane, and his kisses don't even begin to compare to yours. They're not even the same thing."

Reece grunted, apparently pleased.

"So how long is this kiss-ban of yours going to last?" he asked in a bruised-sounding tone. From this distance I could no longer see his face, but I knew he was pouting.

"As long as it takes. I don't like it any more than you do." My tone softened. "You know I want you, but I could never be happy with just fooling around with you or having cheap sex behind Imogen's back. As long as you're under her rule, you're not free to be my mate. I love you too much to be anything else to you."

"I love you, too," he said, sounding resigned. "But for the record, I would have settled for the cheap sex in the meantime."

I couldn't help it—I laughed. "You're incorrigible."

"And you're gorgeous. And sweet. And sexy. And you're going to drive me insane before we get to Canada and get back home again." He let out a surprising roar and gripped the bedsheets so hard they ripped.

When I stopped laughing, I said, "I'm sorry. It's not easy for me, either. I've wanted you for so long, but we have to be patient. Sadie will know what to do. She'll help us."

Reece was quiet for so long I thought he'd fallen asleep, but then he spoke, sounding as wide awake as I was.

"What if there's another answer?"

"What do you mean?" I asked.

"What if Imogen *wasn't* queen anymore?"

"She'll never give up the throne—not for a few thousand more years anyway."

"I wasn't talking about voluntarily." He shifted, pushing up to an elbow and turning toward me. "I'm going to tell you something you're not going to like—and then I'm going to suggest something I hope you'll like very much."

"I'm listening."

"Okay, first for the bad news." Reece hesitated but went

on. "My mission isn't to gain an audience with Sadie and ask for her cooperation and partnership. It was at first—that's the mission I initially suggested to Imogen before the bombing of the VHC headquarters—but things changed. Imogen sent me to assassinate Sadie."

I sat bolt upright in bed, so stunned I could barely breathe, much less respond. Minutes earlier I had been making out with Reece. We'd probably have been making love right now if I hadn't put a stop to things. And all along he'd been planning to kill my mentor? I felt sick.

"You were going to use *me* to get close to her."

"I know you're upset," he said quickly. "Just hear me out. I never felt great about it, but Imogen's the queen, and I didn't really think I had a choice. And accepting the mission was the only way I knew of to get you out of the Bastion and out of Imogen's hands. If it had come down to Sadie's life or yours—well, you know how I feel, so I'm not even going to say it. The point is, I have no intention of going through with it now. Maybe I never would have."

I was still a little bit in shock. "If you *had* gone through with it, I don't know if I could have—"

"We're never going to have to find out, okay? I'm not going to hurt Sadie. I have a better plan. Instead of asking Sadie to join forces with Imogen, who cannot be trusted, we can ask her to help us *overthrow* Imogen."

"And become queen of the Crimson Court?" I said. "She'll say no. She has no interest in that."

"Actually I was going to suggest someone else for the job. You."

My jaw unhinged, falling open. "What? No. That's ridiculous. I may have queen DNA or whatever, but I have no idea what I'm doing. Plus, aren't queens just as forbidden from taking a single mate as drones are? I remember that stuff you told me the night of the Inception Ball. I don't want to mate with a never-ending succession of Bloodbound drones."

"For which I am eternally grateful," Reece said. "But we'll cross that bridge when we come to it. For now we can just take care of the first part of the equation, deposing the tyrannical leader. And who knows? Maybe Sadie will change her mind about the queen thing. She doesn't have the VHC anymore. She's in hiding. She might welcome the opportunity to live in safety and lead the vampire race."

"She would be a fantastic queen," I conceded, starting to get into the idea. This was a plan I could get behind. "Sadie would be so much better for our people. She's selfless, and *she* wouldn't be constantly pressuring me to turn a human. I'd actually be happy to follow in Sadie's footsteps."

"Either way, we can't let Imogen stay on the throne—not if we ever want to be together."

"I do want to be with you, Reece. I hope Sadie will agree to it. What about the Bloodbound, though? Won't they fight for Imogen?"

"You leave that to me. I've been thinking about it. She isn't exactly good to us. The Bloodbound are loyal to her because they have no choice—her queensblood keeps them bound to her. I'm an exception. I guess because she's my maker. It must give me some immunity. But Sadie has queensblood, too, right?"

"Right. She must have if they're sisters. She told me a little about how they were turned—they had the same maker. Oh Reece, I think this could really work."

If Sadie agreed to our plan, Reece could help distribute her blood to the other Bloodbound and turn their loyalty from Imogen to Sadie. Then it would be a simple matter of taking Imogen out.

Simple. Ha. But there had to be a way. And we still had time to think about it.

"How long till sundown?" I asked.

Reece checked the clock. "Two hours. Why?"

"I want to get to Sadie as soon as possible. The sooner we get this plan in motion, the sooner our eternity together can begin."

19

A SWARM OF DRONES

Reece

The weather had cleared by the time we left the hotel that night.

What I saw when we emerged from the building's front door surprised me. We were in Niagara Falls, and from up here on the bluff, the view was amazing.

The view right next to me was even more spectacular. Abbi had put on another of Larkin's provocative outfits, a skin-tight top and micro mini skirt she'd paired with ankle boots and thigh-high socks she said were for warmth.

If she'd meant for *my* warmth, the ensemble was working beautifully. It was all I could do to pry my eyes away from the band of bare skin between the top of the socks and the hem of her skirt and force myself to look at the world-famous geological marvel below us.

I wrapped my coat around her for her sake—and for mine.

"Wow. It's so pretty," Abbi said, craning her neck to see around me. "Look at the lights. Do you think we have time to just walk down and see the falls for a few minutes before we get back on the road?"

"Sure. We're only about five hours from Sudbury now—we'll easily make it there tonight."

Together we walked down the hill toward Queen Victoria Park and its viewing area on the brink of the falls. Standing at the railing, we watched the progression of colored lights dance over the powerful multiple cascades.

The mist rising from them coated Abbi's hair and face, making her look as if she was covered in a layer of tiny gemstones.

She gazed around like a little girl at a Christmas light display. Her mouth was wide open, and she kept laughing and pointing in different directions as she noticed each new aspect of the natural wonder.

She looked over at me with a happy smile, and I sort of lost my breath. "Isn't it so beautiful?"

I reached over and stroked her damp cheek with one finger. "*You* are so beautiful."

"So are you," she said, wrapping her small hand around mine. "I wish I could kiss you right now. Right here in public."

"Soon. Let's get going so we can make that as soon as possible."

We walked back to the car. As we drove away, we passed the falls one last time, and Abbi turned back for a final look.

"I'm really glad I got to see that in person," she said. "I saw it in a book once. Growing up in my community, the library was how I experienced the world. I sort of thought that was as close as I'd ever get."

"Your family didn't travel?"

"Short trips only. Horse drawn buggies aren't meant for long distance."

"Right. My family had an SUV, but we never took any long car trips."

Our mutual longing to get away from home and explore the world was one of the first points of connection Abbi and I had shared, sitting on the hood of my car that night talking about the places we wanted to go.

"You wanted to see Venice before it's completely underwater," she said. "And you wanted to live at the beach someday."

"You remember that?"

"I remember everything about that night." Her tone was faraway. "I've relived it so many times, it's almost like a movie in my mind. Whenever I was lonely or sad or missing you—which was a lot—I played the movie and escaped into a happier time and place."

I reached over and captured her hand, squeezing it. "I hate to think about you being lonely or sad. But I'm glad you missed me. I missed you, too."

Her fingers returned the squeeze, and she gave me a smile so sweet I had to lean over and give her a quick against-the-rules kiss. She gave me a chiding glance but didn't stop smiling.

"I'd still love to live at the beach," I said. "Or at least go there with you and stay for a long, long time."

"Oh my gosh, a hot sunny beach sounds like Heaven right now." Shivering, Abbi pressed a button on the dashboard to turn up the temperature.

"Ontario today, beach later," I said.

"What a tease."

"It's not a tease—it's a promise." I gave her a wink and pulled the car onto the Trans-Canada highway, taking us north once again.

It didn't really matter to me how cold it was. Even if I had to drive another day in a whiteout, it wouldn't have bothered me.

I felt... good. I would have felt *better* had we been able to continue what we had started in that hotel room, but Abbi was right to stop it, of course. We had a do-able plan in place, and it would be stupid to screw it up by tipping Imogen off just before we could execute it.

Abbi and I had waited this long, we could wait a little more. And as she'd said, we'd have eternity to spend together.

It had thrilled me to hear the words coming out of her beautiful mouth. I would never, ever, get tired of hearing her say she loved me. And with Sadie on the Crimson throne, we could finally *be* together.

I'd also be free of the threat of forced sexual servitude. Some of the guys hadn't minded. They thought Imogen was hot, and some of them even vied for her attention.

Kannon wasn't one of them, but it didn't seem to bother him much either. After what had happened with his human ex-girlfriend, he'd given up on the whole concept of love, so he said a meaningless tumble with Imogen every once in a while was no big deal.

"Do you think with Sadie as the queen of the Crimson court, the Bloodbound will be necessary anymore?" Abbi asked as if reading my mind.

I shrugged. "I don't know. I don't think it's a bad idea to maintain a security force, but maybe an army wouldn't be necessary anymore. I can't see Sadie suddenly deciding to lead an armed rebellion against the human government."

"No. Definitely not. She'll still want to use diplomacy. A united front and greater numbers will be a good thing, though—if she can persuade the citizens of the Bastion that peace is a better solution. What about the Bloodbound's *other* function?"

"You mean as queen bee baby-daddies?" I joked. "I'm not sure. Sadie is as old as Imogen. As far as I know she's never produced a biological child, has she?"

"No."

"Right. So, I don't know... I guess that's always the goal, to be able to continue the species without biting humans. Which means Sadie will want an heir—someone younger and more fertile, someone with great queen DNA."

"You can stop right there. I'm not going to be summoning a different soldier to my chambers every night."

I grabbed her hand, squeezing it in mine. "Good. That was a test, by the way."

It was a few minutes before *I* could summon the guts to ask my next question. "I just wondered if maybe... you know, you were maybe hoping to have kids. Because if so, that's your only chance of conceiving. Imogen said it works the same as it does with those killer bees. It takes a swarm of drones..."

Abbi interrupted me. "The only swarm of drones I'd be interested in would be a yardful of little boys who looked just like *you*. Since that's not in the cards, we'll just have to settle for it being the two of us forever."

Lacing my fingers with hers, I lifted her hand to my lips and kissed it. "Sounds good to me."

For a few minutes we were both quiet.

"It would've been nice to have children, though, wouldn't it?" I said. "Myself, I picture three little girls. All of them look exactly like you."

Abbi grinned ear to ear. "Three girls. I always knew you were brave. I didn't think you were stupid."

2 0

SHE WAS HERE

Abbi

We reached Sudbury with plenty of dark to spare.

Imogen's awareness of her sister's life force had pointed us in the direction of Ontario. It had been intelligence from a network of her vampire sources that had narrowed our target to Sudbury—specifically to a research lab owned by the National Public Health Agency.

After Canada had offered Sadie sanctuary, she'd apparently gotten right back to work. The report said some researchers there had been attempting to create a viable substitute for human blood and had gotten quite close.

Sadie had reportedly brought an American vampire scientist with her, and they were trying to help speed the process.

It was as good a place as any to start.

"What are the chances she'll actually be at the lab?" I asked Reece.

"Slim. But someone there might know where Sadie is staying or if she's set up a new VHC headquarters here in the local area. It's our only lead, so I hope it pans out."

We parked in front of the dark building. A few cars were parked outside it, but there were no lights visible through the windows and glass front door.

"Looks like it's closed," I said.

"Yeah. Which is weird for a vampire facility at night. Today's not a holiday in Canada, is it?"

"I don't think so. Maybe it's not a vampire facility. Maybe the staff are humans."

"Humans working on a blood substitute? I guess it's possible. It *is* in their best interests to find a viable alternate food source for vampires. Come on, let's see if it's locked."

The front door opened easily, and we stepped inside. Motion-activated lighting blinked on, illuminating the lobby area.

"Okay, well that answers that then," Reece said. "They're open. Maybe they don't staff the front desk at night. The overnight employees must be back in the lab area."

Together we walked down a hall lined with office doors. It was eerily quiet. My guess was this facility operated like many that had a mix of human and vampire employees. The humans worked during the day, and the vampires worked overnight.

Unfortunately, it was the front office workers who were more likely to be able to give us Sadie's contact information.

"Doesn't it seem strange that there's no security?" I asked.

"Yes. It does." Reece drew a dagger from beneath his jacket and held it in a ready position.

At the end of the hall, we finally spotted a light. It was coming from beneath a closed door with a sign that read Hematology Lab.

Reece tapped on the door with the tip of his knife, and we waited.

"Hello? Enrique?" a female voice called. "I thought you weren't coming in tonight."

The sound of footsteps was followed by the door opening. On the other side stood a very surprised looking female vampire. My own jaw dropped open, mirroring hers.

"Larkin?"

"Abigail?" she asked, wide-eyed.

Larkin looked from me to Reece and back to me again. Her lips split into a wide smile.

"What on earth are you doing here? Where have you *been*?" Her gaze dropped to my outfit. "Are those my Fangers clothes?"

I laughed out loud, and we hugged. "It's a long story. I'll tell you everything. But first, what are *you* doing here? This is Reece by the way."

"Hi Reece. Larkin Spurling." She shook his hand then turned back to me. "I've been working here since the bombing at the VHC. Some people helped me and Sadie get out of the country, and we came up here to continue our work. She set me up in a lab in LA working on a special project, but after the explosion, we didn't think it was safe to keep using it. I would have told you, but I haven't been able to reach you."

"I was in prison—the Safety Center in Merced. I escaped and went to your apartment in San Francisco, which is why I'm wearing your clothes, and then to the Bastion and—well like I said, it's a long story. So Sadie *is* here then? We came here looking for her."

Larkin's smile crumpled. "She *was* here. Abbi... Sadie's dead."

21

MASTERPIECE

Abbi

It was like a bear trap snapped closed around my heart. The spasm of pain was so intense I nearly doubled over.

"Dead?"

Though Larkin had spoken clearly, the word made no sense to me. Sadie Aldritch couldn't be dead. It was impossible.

Reece reached out to steady me as I swayed on my feet. My brain felt like a shaken snow globe, the thoughts and feelings a dizzying whirl.

Unable to manage a full sentence, I whispered, "How?"

"She was killed two days ago," Larkin said. "House fire. I'm so sorry."

"Do they know if it was arson?" Reece demanded.

"Are you sure she was in the house?" I asked, hanging on to a sliver of hope.

Larkin nodded her head sadly. "The fire department found the body. It was a lake house on Lake Wanapitei—the owners didn't use it in the winter and let Sadie stay there rent-free. The fire investigator said it might have been caused by a faulty wood stove, but I don't think so. Earlier this week, Sadie said she thought she was being followed. Two nights ago when she didn't answer her phone, I was worried about her. I drove out there to check on her and saw the firetrucks. The place was an inferno."

The mental image was too much for me. I broke down in sobs and turned toward Reece, who wrapped his arms around me and pulled me against his chest.

Larkin's hand rested on my back. "I'm so sorry," she repeated. "I know you two were close. I'm devastated, too. She was looking for you, you know? She was very worried about you when you stopped coming into work at the VHC. I wish she could see that you're okay. She'd be so relieved."

"I just can't believe it. She was so good, so kind. What are we going to do without her?" I said.

Larkin's voice quavered. "I honestly don't know. I haven't been able to think of anything else, but I came in to work tonight because I know that's what Sadie would have wanted me to do. We're so close to a cure. I can't stop now. I want to finish the work—for her."

Reece's voice rumbled against my cheek as he spoke to Larkin over my head. "A cure? For what?"

"For vampirism," she said as if it should have been obvious. "That's what Sadie had me working on in LA and then continuing at the lab here."

"Wow," he said. "A vampirism cure. I never thought it was possible."

"As it turns out, it's more possible than creating artificial human blood," Larkin said. "Or, at least, it's a bit easier. They've been trying to create a viable blood substitute since the 1970s, and still, scientists can't come up with one that really works. But the cure... we've actually got a formula ready for testing on live vampires."

We all went to the laboratory's lounge and took seats,

Reece and I sitting together on a low vinyl couch and Larkin selecting the club chair opposite it. I tried to focus on the conversation, though snippets of memories about Sadie and conversations we'd shared kept stealing into my brain and pulling me out of the moment.

"We listened to news radio just yesterday and heard no mention of her death," Reece was saying when I tuned back in.

"There are some pretty high-ranking vampires in the government here. They agreed to help keep it quiet for a few more days until it's determined whether the fire was truly accidental or if it was intentionally set," Larkin explained.

"Sadie was a hero to many vampires here as well as in America," she said. "When word gets out there will be a lot of grieving. But if it's learned she was murdered, there could be uprisings, violence. Vampires could get killed. We have to make sure we have all the facts and put together a plan for how the information is released."

"Yes," Reece said in a thoughtful voice. "If someone wanted to spark a revolt, the assassination of a beloved vampire leader would be one way to go about it. The VHC bombing didn't get the job done, so maybe they decided to try again."

I lifted my head to look at his face. "You think Imogen is behind it? You think she sent someone else here to kill Sadie?"

"Maybe," he said. "She might have suspected—and rightly so—that my plans had changed. But Sadie had a lot of enemies. Her sister was only one of them. The anti-vamp extremists are growing more and more aggressive, and they aren't limited to one country. President Parker didn't help things, though. He's high on my list of likely suspects."

"You think *he* had her assassinated?" Larkin asked.

"I don't know if he was directly involved or whether he

inspired it, and it was just some nutjob who carried it out in response to all the fire-and-brimstone rhetoric. Either way, I'm betting that arson investigator's report will turn up some accelerants. A 'faulty wood stove' right on the heels of a terrorist bombing is just too coincidental."

"I'm worried about you now," I told Larkin. "I don't think you're safe here. If someone followed Sadie, they probably know this lab is connected to her work."

She grimaced. "I've thought about that. I even advised the other researchers and staff who use this building to take a few days off just in case. But I hated to stop when we're so close. This is the culmination of my life's work—it's my masterpiece. And the Canadian government promised us a lot of willing vampire volunteers to test the formula when it was ready. I was just about to get the trials started."

"How much time would you need for that?" Reece asked.

"A few weeks maybe? I mean, it would probably take only days to work, but I'd need to replicate the results in lots of vampires before it could be offered to the general public as a cure."

Glancing over at Reece, I saw my grim thoughts mirrored in his face. "We don't have weeks," I told Larkin.

Imogen had made it clear if the two of us didn't return—with haste—my friends Kelly and Heather would pay the price. They might be imprisoned or maybe even killed. Shane would definitely die.

If Sadie were here, she could have helped us think of a way around it. She might have even agreed to be part of our coup and replace Imogen as the queen of the Crimson Court.

As things stood, there was no other choice. We had to go back.

After a moment Reece said, "I know of a place with a large supply of test subjects. How soon could you be ready to travel?"

"The formula is stable enough to move now—all it needs is a cooler with some ice packs—but I'd have to leave all my equipment. It's too much to transport on short notice," Larkin said.

"Pack up what you can and be ready to leave at first dark tomorrow night. Just tell us what to do, and we'll help you. Then I think all of us should get some sleep. We've got a long drive ahead of us."

22

GOOD NEWS AND BAD NEWS

Reece

Larkin went home to pack her personal belongings and gave us her address so we could pick her up at nightfall.

Abbi and I spent the daylight hours in a hotel. This time, we slept.

On the way to Larkin's cottage that night, Abbi seemed consumed by her thoughts.

"You doing okay over there?" I asked. "Thinking about Sadie?"

"Actually, I was just thinking about Imogen. Do you really think she's going to be okay with us bringing a vampire 'cure' to the Bastion? I know her, and I'm pretty sure she doesn't see vampirism as something to be cured. She *loves* being a vampire. If it wouldn't mean the end of our food supply, she'd be happy for vampires to take over the entire world and let humans go extinct."

"I think you're absolutely right on that last part. As far as whether Imogen will approve of the cure or not, it doesn't really matter. Whether she loves it or hates it, she's going to *want* it—in *her* possession. And you can bet she already knows about it. So we have no choice. We have to take it to her. Or else."

"Larkin will be heartbroken if Imogen destroys the formula she's worked so hard on. She called it her masterpiece."

"I don't see that we have any choice—not if you want Kelly, Heather, and Shane to keep their respective heads on their respective shoulders."

"Point taken. Larkin can just recreate the formula... maybe. Actually I don't know that much about science, so I'm not sure if that's even possible."

"We'll have to take the chance."

When we arrived at Larkin's address, it was immediately obvious something was wrong. Her front door stood wide open, and the glass in it was broken.

"Oh my God," Abbi wheezed.

We both got out of the car and ran for the cottage, calling Larkin's name. Inside we found more glass on the floor and other signs of a struggle.

"Stay right behind me," I said to Abbi, extending an arm to prevent her from moving past me and farther into the house.

Drawing my weapon, I moved from room to room, alert and ready in case the intruder—or intruders—were still here.

There was no one, and it was a good thing because when we reached the kitchen I wouldn't have been able to keep Abbi behind me no matter what. Larkin was lying on the floor bleeding from a head wound.

"She's been shot," I said.

Both of us knelt at her side.

"Larkin. Larkin, can you hear me?" Abbi said. Tears streamed down her face at the sight of her friend's grave wound.

Larkin wasn't dead. I could hear her heartbeat. It was weak but there.

I pushed up my sleeve, preparing to rip my wrist open and offer Larkin my blood, but Abbi stopped me.

"No. Let me."

She bit her own wrist and placed it at Larkin's mouth. Her friend drank, feebly at first then with increasing energy and enthusiasm.

After a minute, I said, "That's enough. You'll weaken yourself."

Abbi shot me an annoyed look. "I don't care about that. She needs it."

Grabbing her arm, I pulled it away from Larkin's lips. "*I* care. She's had enough. Her pulse is strong now. She's going to be okay."

Sure enough, within minutes, the bullet pushed its way to the surface of her skull and fell to the floor. A few minutes later Larkin was fully conscious and sitting up.

"Did you get him?"

"No. Did you see who did this?" I asked. "Human or vampire?"

"I'm not... sure. I heard your car stop outside. I was getting ready to take some last-minute stuff out of the fridge. I turned around, and someone was behind me. Male, I'm pretty sure. He shot me before I could get a good look at him."

As if just now thinking of it, she lifted a hand to her forehead and probed the healed wound. "You gave me blood?"

She looked from one to the other of us.

"Abbi did," I said. "How are you feeling?"

"Good. A little woozy still but a lot better than I should be considering I was just shot at point-blank range. Thank you."

Abbi looked embarrassed. "At least this alleged 'queensblood' of mine is good for something."

Now that Larkin was out of danger and thinking clearly, it was time to figure out what was going on.

"Do you think it was an assassination attempt?" I asked, looking around again for signs the cottage had been ransacked.

Larkin shook her head. "I don't know why anyone would want to kill me. It's not like I'm some kind of leader or a famous figure like Sadie. I'm a science nerd—I practically live in the lab."

"It had to be about the cure then. How many people know about it?"

She shrugged. "A handful? It wasn't a secret, but we hadn't published anything about it yet either. We were waiting on the clinical trials so we'd know if it actually worked or not before we contacted the medical journals. Everyone at the lab knew about it, but outside of that, there were probably only a few people, like their significant others."

"Do you have a boyfriend you might have told?" Abbi asked.

"No. No one since Curtis, and I haven't talked to him in a while. He has a new girlfriend."

"I know," Abbi said. "I saw him in San Francisco. He helped us."

"We really do have a lot of catching up to do," Larkin remarked.

"Well, we'll have plenty of time to do it. It's a twelve-hour drive to Northwestern Virginia. You feel okay to travel? Where are your bags?" Abbi asked.

She looked around, obviously planning to carry Larkin's things to the car for her. There were no suitcases or even an overnight bag near the front door or anywhere else I could see.

"Are they in your room?" Abbi asked, standing and turning toward the doorway to the bedroom.

"No. I set them in the foyer so I'd be ready to walk out the door when you arrived. You don't see them?"

Larkin joined me as I walked through the entire cottage, checking to see if she might have placed them somewhere different from where she remembered. There were no packed bags in sight. The house was not ransacked, and she said nothing else seemed to be missing.

"The intruder must have taken them. Wait..." She jogged back into the kitchen and looked around.

"I had a cooler on the island here. I'd just put some blood bags in it for the trip. It's gone, too."

"Your intruder must have come here looking for the cure. You did bring it home from the lab last night, right?" I asked.

"Yes."

"I bet he assumed it was in one of your bags—or the cooler," Abbi said. "So he grabbed them all and ran when he heard us coming."

Larkin smiled. "Well the bad news is that scumbag made off with my Doc Martens and my favorite pair of jeans. The good news is I hadn't packed the formula yet. I was waiting till the last minute to make sure it stayed cold enough."

She opened the refrigerator door and squatted to reach into one of the drawers at the bottom. It was filled with blood bags. Moving them, she grasped something and stood up, turning around with a smile. In her hand were three capped hypodermic needles.

"Ta da!"

"Great. Now I have a little good-news-bad-news scenario for *you*," Abbi said. "Which do you want first?"

"The good news?" Larkin said.

Abbi grinned. "I have some clothes in my suitcase you can wear. I'm *pretty* sure they'll fit."

"And the bad news?"

"They're *your* clothes—the ones from Fangers—and they're really, really slutty."

23
YOU PROMISED ME

Abbi

Larkin and I spent the drive reminiscing about Sadie, and Reece and I tried to prepare her for the Bastion, which she'd never visited.

When we arrived at the caverns, there was something... off. I felt it immediately.

First, the smell of human blood hung in the atmosphere like a heavy fog. And there had been a change in the mood of the place. It had never exactly been "the happiest place on earth," but tonight there was a sinister feeling in the air, a dark, charging energy.

Which was odd considering we hadn't seen anyone yet, apart from the guard at the entrance. He'd waved us through, and Larkin and I had followed Reece down the staircases to the cavern floor. Now we stood surveying the abandoned space.

"Where is everyone?" I asked in a hushed voice.

"I'm not sure. At this time of night, the place should be bustling," Reece said.

A uniformed figure entered the torch-lit chamber from

the far end, striding toward us. As he approached, he pushed back the hood of his black Bloodbound cloak, revealing a head of unmistakable long blond hair.

It was Kannon. He broke into a wide grin. "You're back, brother. And I hear your mission was a huge success."

He and Reece embraced in a quick man-hug then Kannon stepped back and looked at me.

"Good to see you, too, squirt. Who's your..." His booming voice died off into a whisper as his eyes locked with Larkin's. "... friend?"

Kannon stared at her like a man lost in a desert who'd stumbled upon an oasis. Or maybe someone seeing a mirage of an oasis because he stared at her as if she wasn't real. Did they know each other?

Apparently not because she let out a nervous sounding giggle and extended a hand to him. "I'm Larkin Spurling, a friend of Abbi's from California. It's nice to meet you."

Still looking like he was in a daze, Kannon took her hand and shook it. And kept shaking it.

"Kannon," he mumbled. "Friend of Reece. And Abbi's. You've... never been here before, have you?"

She looked up and around at the calcite formations on the ceilings and walls surrounding us. "No. First time. It lives up to the hype—and that's based on just this first chamber. I hear the caverns cover sixty-four acres?"

He nodded. "Yeah. I'll be happy to give you the grand tour later if you'd like."

She beamed. "I'd love that. I guess I should meet your leader first though. Imogen? I have something to show her."

At this his awed expression abruptly changed, as if he'd been yanked out of a pleasant dream by the annoying beep of an alarm clock.

"Yeah... about that..." Kannon turned to Reece. "There's a sort of... party going on in the Grand Dome."

He didn't look thrilled about it.

"A party?" I asked. Was it time for another Inception Ball?

Kannon grimaced and nodded. "Imogen's celebrating."

I looked from his face to Reece's pained expression. What was I not getting? "Celebrating what?"

Reece answered for him. "Sadie's death. I called it in before we left Sudbury."

The bear trap was back, gouging my heart again with its steel jaws. "Imogen is celebrating Sadie's murder by throwing a *party*?"

She had no feeling at all for her sister. She truly was a monster. I wanted to turn around and leave right then, but of course I couldn't do that. I had to get Shane out of here—and ensure that this time Reece would be coming with me.

"It's more like a feast, actually," Kannon clarified. His brow furrowed, and he swallowed hard, as if struggling to keep down a surge of bile. "Imogen sent the Bloodbound out last night to gather some... *provisions*."

We were all quiet for a minute as the implications of his words sank in.

"Do you mean humans?" Larkin asked, apparently just now getting it. "She had a bunch of *humans* brought here? For their blood?"

Kannon nodded grimly. "Everyone's there—the whole population of the Bastion—at Imogen's orders. Things are... I don't even know what to say. Things have kinda gone off the rails in the past couple of days."

He rubbed his forehead and let out a tired-sounding breath before turning to Larkin. "If you're used to Sadie Aldritch's way of doing things, you might want to just go directly to the guest chambers. You probably won't like what you see at the feast."

That's when it hit me. "Kannon... where's Shane? Is he still in the medical clinic?"

Kannon looked down at me with sad eyes. "Sorry squirt. I know you had a soft spot for him, but, you know, he's human, and we had orders—"

"Where is he?" I demanded.

"He's in the Grand Dome. I'm sorry, Abbi. I did try—"

I didn't stick around to hear the rest of his excuse. If he'd let my friend—who'd saved my life—become a human hors d'oeuvre, there wasn't one good enough. I'd never speak to Kannon again.

Taking off at a full sprint, I weaved through the interconnected caverns toward the Grand Dome. The artfully lit stalactites and stalagmites all resembled teeth and jagged knives to me as I passed beneath them in a life-and-death race toward the Bastion's largest community gathering space.

At least I hoped there was a life left to save.

Sweet, kind Shane. How could I have brought him here?

A blur of motion beside me drew my eye. Reece had caught up to me and was running at my side.

"Let me handle it," he said between breaths. "When we get there, let me do the talking."

"You promised me, Reece. You promised me he'd be okay here."

"I know. We don't know anything yet. Let's just wait and see the situation before you assume the worst."

We reached the Grand Dome and threw open its heavy double doors.

What I saw inside was far, far worse than anything I ever could have imagined.

24

A CHOICE TO MAKE

Reece

Red. Everywhere I looked, the Grand Dome's signature white flowstone was stained dark red.

Blood covered the floor, dripped from the walls, and splatters decorated the room's ten-story-tall stone columns, darkening their usual rose-colored tone.

The feast must not have been going on for long because many of the human "guests" were still alive. Screams of terror echoed through the room.

They were punctuated with laughter from some of the vampires who watched their partially drained victims try to escape only to slip and fall in pools of their own blood.

To their credit, many of the vampires in attendance were not participating in the massacre. They stood off to the sides looking troubled, horrified in some cases. A few even cried. Clearly they weren't there of their own will but at Imogen's command.

Reaching for Abbi, I drew her against me, attempting to shield her eyes and turn her away from the nightmarish sight.

Imogen had gone mad. That was the only explanation for this. Now that Sadie was dead, there was no one to challenge her.

No one but Abbi.

I had to get her out of here.

Surveying the macabre scene in front of us, I knew there was no way Abbi would ever agree to be Imogen's heir now—which meant Imogen would see her as nothing but a threat. Which, in turn, meant she'd have no further interest in keeping Abbi alive.

"Let's go." I dragged Abbi back from the doorway. "Let's just turn around and leave right now before anyone spots us. We'll leave the Bastion forever, go on the run. I don't care about the resistance. I don't care about the human race. I only care about you."

She dug her heels in, stopping our motion, and pulled away from me. "What about the Bloodbound? And your vows? I thought you were bound to Imogen. You're always saying we can never escape her."

"My bond with *you* is the strongest thing I've ever felt in my life," I said. "You are my destiny, Abbi. I'll do *anything* to protect you. We may have to stay on the run forever, but I don't care where I am as long as I'm with you."

Her expression was torn. I knew she wanted to be with me, but still her eyes drifted toward the open doors. "What about Shane?"

"I don't care about him either. Chances are he's dead already. There's no need for us to die, too."

"But there's also a chance he's still alive. How can I leave him to be slaughtered? How can *you*?"

"Easily—if it means keeping you safe."

Her face registered shock and horror. "You can't mean that. The Reece I met and fell in love with was a good guy, a caring person. I could never be with someone who doesn't care about anyone else."

It wasn't exactly true. I did care—I just cared about Abbi's life more than all the others combined. And right now hers was in grave danger.

"You're all that matters to me," I said. "I won't apologize for loving you, and I won't let you risk your life for a human who's as good as dead anyway."

"I can't believe what I'm hearing. I made Shane a promise, and I'm going to keep it. I'm going in there—whether you help me or not."

She tried to walk away, and I grabbed her hand, tugging her back toward me.

"Don't," I pleaded. "Stay with me, and we'll leave together. Please, if you love me, just... don't go in there."

"Don't make this an ultimatum," she said in return.

She jerked from my grasp and ran into the room. "Shane," she yelled as her head turned one way then the other. "Shane, I'm here. Where are you?"

Throwing up my hands and blowing out a harsh breath, I followed her. I didn't share her hope that she'd still find the human alive, but I certainly wasn't going to let Abbi wade into the fray alone.

In spite of my claim of not caring about the humans, it was impossible not to feel sorry for them once we were in the middle of the bloodbath. What a horrible way to go.

No one deserved to die this way, not even the guy who'd tried to steal the only girl I'd ever loved.

Speaking of Shane, I didn't see him anywhere—not that any of the humans were exactly recognizable at this point. With me close at her heels, Abbi reached the front of the room near the raised platform where Imogen sat.

The queen calmly observed the spectacle as if it was a garden party and not a portrait of hell's inmates devouring each other. She wore an expression of delight so acute she almost looked insane. Maybe it was *beyond* almost.

When she spotted us, her smile spread. She stood and opened her arms in welcome.

"The victorious warrior returns." Her expression soured. "And my dear daughter. Come join the party, children. There's plenty for everyone."

Abbi strode up to her. "Where's Shane?"

Imogen's lips pursed, and she raised one brow, directing a significant glance behind us. "I believe he's on the dessert table."

Abbi and I both whirled around.

Shane's body was indeed stretched out on a stone table about thirty feet away. He was motionless and covered in bite marks and streaks of blood. About ten vampires swarmed around him. Who knew how many had already bitten him?

We were too late. He was either going to turn or die.

It looked like it was going to be the latter. He was pale, his face and body looking sunken.

Abbi rushed toward him, pushing away the other vampires. Some of them fought back until Imogen's order rang through the chamber.

"Stop. Let her have the boy."

The other vampires backed away obediently, and Abbi moved close to Shane. Tears streamed down her cheeks as she catalogued his wounds and brushed his hair back from his unconscious face.

"Shane. Can you hear me? Shane?" She bit her own wrist, holding the bleeding wound over his still mouth.

"I'm afraid he's beyond the point of healing, my dear," Imogen taunted. "He's lost quite a bit of blood—almost all of it actually."

She descended the stairs and strolled toward us. "You

have a choice to make. You can bite him and turn him... or you can let him die."

Fire blazed in Abbi's eyes. "I can't. I can't do either of those things. You *promised* he'd remain unharmed if I did what you wanted, if I helped Reece get in touch with Sadie."

Imogen grinned. "But you *didn't* keep your end of the bargain, did you?"

"I tried. Sadie was already dead when we got there. That isn't my fault."

Imogen shrugged. "It isn't mine either."

"Isn't it?" Abbi demanded.

Imogen just laughed. "It doesn't matter. The end result is the same. Besides, his blood smells so lovely, doesn't it? I'm not sure how you can stand so close and resist it. In fact, I think I might just finish him off."

Abbi threw out her palm. "Stay back. Stay away from him. All of you."

She turned back to Shane, crying harder now. "I'm so sorry. You didn't deserve this."

Standing close behind her, I placed a comforting hand on her shoulder. "He won't even feel your bite. And when he wakes, he'll have you to guide him."

The last thing I wanted was Abbi's human sweetie becoming an immortal who'd be attached to her eternally by an unbreakable bond. But I also couldn't bear to see her suffering like this. At this point, she really didn't *have* a choice.

"No. I'm not going to bite him. I'm going to let him die," she said. "I won't force him to become part of this world."

Shock nearly staggered me. She *wasn't* going to turn him?

I hadn't thought there could be anything worse than having him hanging around for the rest of our eternal lives, but this was it. Considering how guilty Abbi felt over Josiah, I had no doubt she'd punish herself for Shane's death forever.

Stroking his hands and face, Abbi said her goodbyes. "I'll never forget you. I'll never forget what you did for me. And I promise... I will mourn you... always."

That's it.

Without waiting for another of Shane's slow heartbeats to pass, I stepped forward and grabbed his bare arm, sinking my teeth deeply into the flesh. I didn't drink, though. Thirst had nothing to do with my motivations.

Abbi gasped, frozen in shock. "Why did you do that?"

"Don't you know?"

She shook her head. "He's going to turn now. He's going to be a vampire."

"That's right. He won't die. I told you—I'd do anything to protect you, including saving you from the guilt. That is, as long as he's not too far gone."

We both looked to Imogen. She lifted a milky white shoulder and let it fall.

"We shall see if he still had sufficient blood left to make the transition." Curling her lip at Abbi, she added, "If he does wake, perhaps he can be your mate."

She looked highly amused at the prospect, flicking a knowing glance at me then Abbi, daring either of us to object.

Abbi turned to me with wide eyes. "Is *that* why you did it? So he wouldn't be bound to me? You turned him out of... of jealousy? What will you do when he wakes? Recruit him to join the Bloodbound so *he* can't take a mate either?"

"No," I shouted. "Maybe. I don't know. When he wakes—*if* he wakes—you can decide what to do with him. Take him as your mate if that's what you want. If you tell me that's what you want, I'll use The Pull on him and command him to love you for eternity."

She covered her face with both hands. "I don't know what I want. I can't believe you did this."

25

TEST SUBJECT NUMBER ONE

Abbi

I'd promised Shane safety and freedom—*that* was what I had wanted for him. If he woke a vampire, those things would be impossible.

Looking at him lying there so pale and lifeless, I doubted he'd wake up at all.

I shouldn't have left him here. But if I hadn't agreed to go on Imogen's mission, I would have lost both him *and* Reece.

Maybe I still had. Reece had *bitten* him—knowing Shane would turn. I clutched my stomach, still in disbelief. His unexpected move to take the decision out of my hands had shocked me to my core.

My only hope was that Larkin's experimental formula would work—if Shane did wake up. And if she hadn't been thrown out of the Bastion already.

But no, there she was, coming this way with Kannon. Of course Imogen's loyal soldier would decide to bring the newcomer—and her special cargo—to his queen.

Imogen hadn't noticed them yet. She had come to stand

by my side—far too close for my comfort. Like mine, her gaze was on Shane.

"He looks quite peaceful now," she mused. "So young and innocent." There was a beat before she continued. "Much like your friend, Josiah."

I whipped my head around to face her. "Josiah?"

I didn't think she'd even noticed Josiah at the accident scene—well, as anything more than a source of blood. My memories of that night were muddled, but they included hearing her tell the rest of her traveling group they were welcome to drink from everyone there but me and Reece, whom she'd claimed.

"He would have made a terrible vampire," she drawled. "And he was definitely dragging *you* down. He didn't even leave his room while his parents screamed and fought for their lives downstairs, just cowered behind that flimsy locked door, mumbling his pathetic prayers."

Reece had told me Imogen had somehow been able to see through his eyes, describing the Yoder's farm and the murder scene in detail when she'd told him he was responsible for it. Was her "vision" really that good?

Then she gave me a smile that lifted the baby hairs on the back of my neck.

"When I dragged him outside and staked him to the ground to await the sunrise, he didn't even fight back. He didn't make a peep. You ran right past him, in fact," she said to me.

Wait... what? When *she* staked him to the ground? My chest tightened, and I blinked repeatedly.

"*You* were there that night?" Reece asked, clearly as dumbfounded as I was.

Imogen laughed. "You didn't really think the farm boy had enough courage to daylight himself, did you? I have to say the incineration did a nice job hiding the evidence. Wooden stakes burn just as thoroughly as vampire flesh."

"So it was *you* who killed Josiah," I said. "And his parents. And you let Reece believe he did it. He joined the Bloodbound out of guilt over that."

She giggled. "I know. Clever, huh? I got one hell of a soldier out of the deal. And I removed *both* impediments to your rightful path to queendom."

Gesturing to Shane's battered body, she said, "Now I've removed a third. Shall we keep going, or are you finally ready to come to your senses and take your place as my heir apparent?"

"You are pure evil. You're *not* my mother, and there is nothing you could teach me that I'd want to learn. You had Sadie killed, too, didn't you? Didn't you?" Enraged, I flew at her.

Either it was the element of surprise or I didn't know my own strength, but I was easily able to overcome Imogen, grabbing her by the throat and pushing her up against one of the large stone columns.

She stared at me with shocked eyes, her mouth open wide but unable to speak with my left hand choking off her air supply. My right hand was poised directly over her heart, ready to strike and rip it out if she fought back.

The members of her personal guard were scattered throughout the room, all in a state of bloodlust and participating fully in the feast. If they were still even capable of rational thought, they probably assumed Reece had the queen covered. He and Kannon were the only two Bloodbound soldiers close enough to see what was happening.

"Abbi—what are you doing?" Kannon yelled, rushing up to me.

I threw out a hand toward him and tightened the one

wrapped around Imogen's trachea, ensuring she wouldn't be able to utter an order he'd be compelled to obey.

"Stay back. I'm warning you—don't come any closer. This has to stop, Kannon, and you know it."

Reece put a hand on his shoulder. "She's right. Things can't go on the way they have been. We all know it. And a challenge is part of the natural cycle with queens. Let them work it out. You know Abbi—she's not going to kill Imogen."

Kannon looked uncertain but complied.

Which left the decision in my hands. What was I going to do here? With a little more pressure, I *could* end Imogen's eternal life. It would cost me my own, which naturally I didn't want, but what else could I do? She was incapable of remorse or rehabilitation, and I couldn't let her keep hurting people.

Not the humans, not the vampires under her rule.

"You're not fit to lead a sing-a-long, much less a community of endangered refugees," I said, gesturing with my free hand toward the carnage surrounding us. "*This*—is not a solution."

She forced out a harsh whisper, spittle flying from her mouth. "Neither is peace. If you're so smart—what *is* the answer?"

"I'm not sure, but it's not ordering your loyal soldiers to kidnap a roomful of innocent humans to be slaughtered."

"They're not loyal," she hissed. "If they were, you'd be in pieces right now. Soon enough, though. You may be physically strong, but your spirit is weak, like Sadie's. I was wrong about you."

Darting her eyes at Kannon and Reece, she said, "I will have their heads. And yours, you ungrateful little—"

Imogen's words cut off abruptly as Larkin dashed forward and plunged a hypodermic needle into her chest.

Kannon whipped around to face her, in shock. "What did you just do?"

Larkin tilted her chin up at him, completely unrepentant. "People were talking about looking for a solution."

She held up the empty needle. "I just happened to have one in my pocket."

"Is that the cure?" Reece asked.

"I guess we'll find out," Larkin said. "Imogen just became test subject number one."

26

PERFECT FOR THE JOB

Abbi

It had been four days since the horrifying feast, and still Shane hadn't awakened. Maybe he'd lost too much blood after all.

I sat by his bedside in the clinic where Dr. Coppa had offered to watch over him. Apparently the staff had gotten attached to my human friend in the time he'd spent here recovering from his gunshot wound.

A couple of them had even offered to guide him through the early stages of vampire life when he woke up.

If he woke up.

I closed my eyes and rubbed my temples, hunching over in the uncomfortable chair.

"I always thought he'd make a good vampire," confessed Ellie, who'd been his primary nurse during his recovery. With a silly eyebrow waggle, she added, "I told all my friends how hot he'd be if he ever turned."

She buzzed about the room, checking the readout on the devices attached to my unconscious friend.

"Have you ever seen anyone take this long to transition?"

I asked. Honestly, Shane looked dead to me, though the instruments indicated brain activity and a weak pulse.

"Not personally, but I heard about a case where it took a couple weeks."

In the room next door, Imogen lay comatose and guarded by Kannon, though it was unclear whether he was there to protect her while she slept—or the rest of us should she wake.

Reece popped into the clinic occasionally to check on both patients. He was gruff and moody, like he had been when he'd first pledged himself to service with the Bloodbound.

As he had on his previous visits, he seemed annoyed to see me standing vigil over Shane today.

"Anything yet?" he asked in a begrudging tone.

"No. He's pretty much the same. How is Imogen?"

"Still sleeping. She hasn't desiccated or anything if that's what you're wondering. Still can't tell if the supposed 'cure' did anything or not."

"Well, if it's 'not,' I'm pretty sure the answer will come in the form of our heads being suddenly disconnected from our bodies."

He nodded then let out a frustrated-sounding noise. "You can't just keep sitting here day and night. It isn't healthy." He tossed a hand in Shane's direction. "There's no telling how long it's going to take for him to wake up. He was almost completely drained."

"I know. I just want to be here when he does. His last minutes of consciousness must have been sheer terror. He's bound to be afraid when he comes to. He needs to see a friendly face."

Reece frowned. "'He needs. He needs,'" he repeated in a mocking tone. "What about what *you* need? Wearing yourself out and making yourself sick isn't going to do him any good.

Dr. Coppa will send word to you as soon as he wakes up. Or I will."

I smirked. "Sure, you will. You made it quite clear you don't care about the humans—especially him."

"I didn't mean it," Reece said. "I only said it because I was trying to keep you from rushing into the Grand Dome and getting yourself killed."

He tugged at my arm, trying to pry me from the chair I'd practically fused with in the past few days. "Come on, I'll walk you back to your quarters. You need to get some rest so you'll be ready to face your new subjects. They'll want to hear from you soon."

I'd been tugging back, resisting him, but I froze in mid-pull. "What do you mean?"

"The Crimson throne is yours now—at least until Imogen wakes and we find out if she's still a vampire. If she isn't, then someone has to rule."

"Well, it won't be me. I don't know anything about leading people."

"Look, Imogen's incapacitated. Sadie is dead. The world outside is a mess. This place is in an uproar—rumors flying everywhere about what really happened during the feast and why no one's seen Imogen. Kannon and I gave the Bloodbound orders to keep the peace, but it won't last long without leadership. Our people need a queen, and you're perfect for the job."

"No—" I tried to protest.

He cut me off. "Yes. You learned diplomacy at Sadie's feet, and you're Imogen's child. You clearly inherited her power— or did you not notice your own strength the other night when you stood up to her? Besides, you're the only one who has the pheromone thing necessary to lead a hive."

Everything he said was true. It was also terrifying.

"I... can't think about it right now, not until Shane wakes

up and I know if he's a vampire or not. And until I know whether the cure will work for him."

Reece didn't like that answer. "I should have let the stupid human die. What kind of idiot makes sure the competition stays around?" he muttered as he turned and left the room, clearly sulking.

I was disappointed in his attitude toward the human race, but then he *had* saved my friend's life. Based on his parting remark, he was misreading my concern for Shane's well-being as something more than friendship.

After Shane woke and I was sure he'd be okay, I'd have to go find Reece and straighten things out with him.

The door opened again, and I thought I'd get the chance sooner than expected, but it wasn't Reece standing in the doorway. It was a young female vampire. She was lovely, with smooth brown skin and a short, curvy build.

"Hi," she said shyly. "Are you Abigail?"

"Yes. Hi. Can I help you?" I darted my eyes over at Shane's helpless form, suddenly feeling protective.

The young woman's gaze went to him, too, and there was a rush of blood to her face. Her eyes filled with tears.

"Wow," she breathed. "It really is him." Stepping farther into the room she said, "I'm an old friend of Shane's. One of my friends is friends with Ellie, who's a nurse here at the clinic. My name is Marjorie."

A fluttery feeling of euphoria lifted my stomach. *"You're* Marjorie?"

"You've heard of me?" she asked with a growing smile. "Did Shane... did he mention me?"

I returned her smile. "Yes. He spoke of you when we were traveling here together from California. He said you were once very important to each other. Would you like to see him?"

"Oh, yes. That would be wonderful."

I gestured for her to come closer, and she hurried across the room to Shane's bedside. She gazed down at him with such obvious affection and concern I wished he were awake to see it.

"Do you live here at the Bastion?" I asked her after a few minutes.

She turned to me as if just remembering there was another person in the room. "Yes. I came here about a year ago after breaking up with my boyfriend—not Shane—the guy I dated after him. Actually, I went looking for Shane before I came here. His house had been sold, and no one knew where his family had moved."

She blushed again. "We dated in high school, but his parents disapproved. I guess I wanted to see him again and see how he felt now that we were both older and more independent. But I couldn't find him..."

Her eyes went back to the sleeping guy. "When I heard my friend talking about Ellie's human patient from California, and that he was bitten by an Arch Vampire, and that his name was Shane Eastwood, I dropped everything and literally ran here."

She turned to me, hugging her own ribcage tightly. "Do you think he'll wake up?"

I stood and placed a comforting hand on her arm. "I believe he will. And when he does, I think you two will have a lot to talk about. He never got over you, you know."

Her eyes glistened again, and she seemed to swallow back a lump in her throat. "I never got over him either. He was the love of my life. Do you think... will he be sad to be a vampire when he wakes up?"

"I'm not sure yet," I said. "If he is, we have a possible cure for him. It could reverse the transformation."

But now I wasn't so sure he'd even want to take it. Once

he was reunited with Marjorie, Shane might want to *stay* a vampire so he could be with her eternally.

Things were certainly not turning out the way I'd expected them too.

"Could I..." Marjorie started, faltered, then spoke again. "Would it be okay if I sat with him? Just for a little while? I know you're close, but, well it would be amazing to be here when he wakes up."

I gestured toward the chair where I'd spent so many hours thinking the same thing. "Please. You're welcome to stay as long as you like. I have a feeling when he opens his eyes, it's *your* face he'd rather see."

And now that Shane was no longer alone, now that there was someone else to watch over him who truly cared about him, I decided to take Reece's advice and get some rest. I left the clinic and walked to my chambers, thinking.

As for the other thing he'd said—about me addressing my "subjects" and ruling the Bastion in Imogen's place, I wasn't sure what to think. Or to do.

If only Sadie were here.

She'd definitely know what to do. She could take over and lead the vampire race, or at least teach me how to.

As it was, I had nothing but some iffy pheromones, a few vampire preparedness classes, and a year working an entry-level job at the Vampire-Human Coalition.

I wasn't even that great of a vampire. How could I be the queen of all of them?

WILLING CONSORT

Abbi

After a long bath, I fell into my bed in the guest suite, mentally and physically exhausted.

I'd barely settled under the covers when there was a knock at the door. I almost didn't answer but thought better of it. It might be something about Shane—or Imogen.

When I opened the door, Reece stood on the other side.

"Hi."

He'd calmed down since the last time I saw him, and it looked like he'd just showered. Instead of his Bloodbound uniform he wore jeans and a dark t-shirt. His dark hair was still damp, and he smelled like cedar and soap.

"Hi. Is everything okay?" I asked.

"I don't know how to answer that, since it kind of depends on you. Could I come in?"

Once inside my room, Reece shifted from foot to foot, looking around and clearing his throat.

"What's going on?" I prompted.

His gaze finally met mine. "I came to apologize. I've been horrible the past few days."

"They've been difficult for all of us," I started, already forgiving him.

He held up a hand. "Let me finish please. I'm sorry for what I said back there in the clinic. I don't hate the whole human race, and I don't want... *Shane* to die."

It looked like it pained him to say Shane's name, but I gave him points for effort.

"And I'm sorry for taking the decision out of your hands back in the Grand Dome," he said. "He's your friend. I should have let you have the final word on the matter."

"It's okay." I meant it. Reece had obviously been thinking with a clearer head than I had during the horrific feast.

"You were right. If you'd left it up to me, Shane would be dead now," I admitted. "At least this way he still has a chance at life. And you were only trying to help."

Reece's face crinkled. "Yeah... see, I have something to confess. I was only helping myself. I didn't want you to 'mourn him always.' Shane came between us enough while he was alive—I wasn't going to let him do it in death."

"Oh."

"I'm selfish when it comes to you," Reece confessed. "Everything I do—everything I've done since I came here was about the chance to be with you. I joined the Bloodbound so I could be with you when you took over for Imogen someday."

He took me in his arms and stroked his fingers down my cheek as if my skin was the softest silk and he couldn't resist touching it.

"That 'someday' is almost here. You're *going* to be queen, Abbi. And I'll be your willing consort—as often as I get the chance." He took a deep breath and steeled his jaw. "The only problem is I'm not sure how I'm going to share you with the other Bloodbound."

"I don't want any of them," I told him. "I don't want anyone but you—ever."

Reece smiled, wide and genuine and with enough warmth to melt even the iciest pocket of resentment I'd been hanging on to.

"I was hoping you'd say that. It's impossible, of course, but I like hearing you say it anyway."

He sank a big hand into my hair and cradled the back of my head, guiding my mouth to his.

I made a half-hearted attempt to pull away. "Maybe we shouldn't..."

"Shut up and kiss me," Reece growled, continuing his sweet assault on my mouth and backing me toward the nearby bed.

As we tumbled onto it, I pulled my mouth away again—though I *really* didn't want to. His kisses were like the richest dessert and the most addictive drug rolled into one. "Are you sure we should—"

"Yes."

Reece yanked his shirt over his head then started working on the buttons of my pj top. "I love you, Abbi. I may not be your last, but by God I'm *going* to be your first. You're going to be my first and *only*—and I plan to make sure you'll think only of *me*, even when those other drones come calling."

I wanted to protest that there would be no other "drones," that even if Imogen died or abdicated her rule, I had no intention of taking her place—on the Crimson throne *or* in the queen's royal bedchamber.

But I didn't say any of it. All I could manage was a breathless, "yes." And then my mouth, and the rest of me, were quite busy for the next several hours.

* * *

Rolling onto his back, Reece pulled me against him, tucking me between his arm and chest.

I wrapped my arm around him and held him close, not wanting the intimate contact to end. Ever. It had been one of the most wonderful experiences of my life. And possibly the stupidest thing I'd ever done.

"We just committed treason," I said, torn between awe and terror.

He pressed his cheek against the top of my head and gave a happy laugh. "No one in the history of time has ever been more thrilled about committing treason than I am. Even if Imogen wakes up a vampire and has me beheaded for it, I still won't be sorry. *That* was worth it."

I slapped at his bare chest. "Don't say that. Don't even joke about it. I can't bear the thought of anything bad happening to you."

He held me tighter. "All the bad has already happened. Now it's time for the good stuff. You're going to be an *amazing* queen."

"Reece... I've told you—I'm *not* going to be queen of the Crimson Court. This doesn't change anything. I still can't fill Imogen's shoes. And I could never live up to Sadie. I'm not enough. I can't do it."

"You don't *have* to do it on your own—I'm here. The Bloodbound are here, and they'll listen to me and Kannon. But you do have to try."

"Do I? I've been thinking... if the cure ends up working on Imogen... we could take it, too. We could be human again."

28

CAN'T GO BACK

Reece

A tremor went through my whole body. I could hardly believe my ears.

"You don't mean that. You're just scared. Either that or my amazing lovemaking skills scrambled that pretty head of yours. You're not thinking straight."

"I *am*. And I do mean it, Reece. I'm a terrible vampire. I'm too... soft."

"You're not soft," I argued, giving her shoulder a gentle squeeze. "You're compassionate. You're one of the strongest people I've ever known... and I live with dozens of huge vampire males. You can be compassionate *and* strong, you know."

She turned her face up to me, her lower lip trembling and her eyes filling, making their color resemble the periwinkles that grew in the meadows where she used to love hiking at night.

"What if I'm not smart enough? I never even graduated from high school."

"You graduated from the school of experience—and your

experiences are far beyond what most people could ever dream of. You love learning, right? You can keep learning. You'll just be doing it on the job. If you ask me, you were born for this."

"I was born to be an Amish farm wife," she countered.

"And yet even then, back when I first met you, I could tell you'd never be satisfied with that. You wanted more, remember? What happened to that girl who wanted a life of excitement and adventure?"

She shrugged and snuggled deeper against me, sounding exhausted. "Maybe too much has happened to her. Maybe she wants to be normal again... to not be a monster."

"You can be a vampire without being a monster. Wasn't that the whole purpose of the VHC—to prove that to people? *You've* proven it. You proved it the night of the feast, and you've been proving it every day you've lived in this existence. You are an example to every vampire out there that it's possible."

"Oh gosh, now you're *really* making me feel like a fraud. No one should look at me for an example of how to live their life."

"If not you, then who? I was mad at you for running into the Grand Dome to try to save Shane with no concern for your own safety, but I have to admit one of the many reasons I love you is that you *do* put others before yourself. That's the best example anyone can set, the willingness to sacrifice yourself for others. That's how I know you'll be a great queen, better than Imogen ever was or ever could be. The people here *need* you. The ones on the outside that were left behind when Sadie died need you."

I paused a beat. "*I* need you."

Abbi rubbed my chest. "I need you, too, Reece. I don't want to give you up."

She lifted her head, and her words poured out faster and

faster. "That's why we both have to take the cure. You could have the life you wanted before all this happened. You could finish your college basketball career, go to law school..."

I stopped her. "Abbi... the life I wanted doesn't exist anymore. Not with what I know now. Not with the way things are going in the world. You know how bad things are. The vampire race *needs* an advocate. They need leadership and protection."

A new light came into her eyes. "Larkin could produce more of the formula—everyone could be cured."

"Even if it's possible for all vampires to be cured, many of them wouldn't want to be," I argued. "A lot of them *can't* go back to their human lives. *I* can't go back. I have no one to go back *to*."

"You'd have me."

"And what about everyone else?" I asked. "Some of our people turned so long ago all their human friends and family are dead now. Some would lose their jobs if they were human again. Some of them would lose more—a mate, a community. Some had incurable diseases before turning. Becoming human again would kill them. What about Kannon? He was a quadriplegic. A human life isn't the end all be all, you know."

She shook her head. "I know. It wasn't perfect, but it was... easier."

"I didn't take you for someone who takes the easy way out. And easier isn't always better. Remember that night under the crimson moon? I said I wanted 'greatness?'"

I stroked her hair back from her face and gave a self-deprecating chuckle. "I felt kind of stupid about it later, and I admit when I believed your life was in danger from Imogen, all I cared about was keeping you alive. But I can see that vision again. *That's* what I want for you, for all of us. You would be a great queen, Abbi."

She shook her head in obvious disbelief. "The words 'queen' and 'Abbi' don't even belong in the same sentence."

"We'll call you Queen Abigail, then," I joked. I leaned my forehead against hers so our eyes were level. "You've grown, you've learned. You've gotten stronger. You may not feel it, but I *see* it in you."

"You're only saying that because you love me."

I chuckled. "I do. But I also believe in you. What will it take to make you believe in yourself?"

"I don't know. I do believe in *us*," she whispered, sounding desperate. "Come with me."

"Stay," I whispered back.

"I'm not sure if I can."

There were tears in her eyes. My heart swelled almost painfully. Pulling Abbi back down to my chest, I pressed a kiss to her hair.

Though she was wrapped in my arms, I felt like she was slipping away from me. She was so convinced she couldn't be the leader the vampire people needed.

The last time she was this certain of something she'd left for California—and left me behind. A sharp spike of fear pierced my heart.

How could I ever live without her? I wanted her more than I'd ever wanted anything in my life. I *loved* her.

For a moment I tried to envision doing what Abbi wanted —taking the cure and going back to being human. I was sure it was the wrong thing. The citizens of the Bastion needed protection and leadership. They needed a queen.

Trying to fill in and be their king wasn't an option. I might have been an Arch Vampire and Imogen's child, but as a male, I lacked the queen bee pheromones necessary to hold a hive together.

But how could I leave the people here—and the entire vampire species—defenseless?

I couldn't.

If the cure worked, and Abbi decided to take it and leave the vampire people behind, I'd have no other choice but to stay and *try* to lead them.

There was a sharp rapping on the door. Abbi slipped from the bed, grabbing her clothes and dressing quickly before answering. She opened the door a crack. On the other side stood one of the clinic staff members.

"He's awake," was all the woman said, but it was enough to send Abbi running down the corridor without taking time to even close the door behind her.

Great. Shane had pulled through, the scrappy little bugger, and she was literally running to him.

So, he was a vampire—and my "child," which meant he'd be hanging around for literally eternity.

The only good thing about the development was the wait was over. Now Abbi would finally be able to think with a clear head and make a decision about her future—and mine.

I honestly didn't know which way she would go.

2 9

THE REAL THING

Abbi

Shane was sitting up in bed and smiling when I arrived. He and Marjorie both turned toward the door.

"Abbi," Shane said in a joyful voice. "Boy am I glad to see you."

"I'm happy to see you, too. How are you? How do you feel?"

"I feel great," he said. "Though I just now figured out I'm actually alive and not in the afterlife. When I woke up and saw Marjorie's face, I wasn't too sure. I thought at first she was here to welcome me to Heaven."

"Awww." She leaned over and squeezed his hand. "You're sweet."

I walked closer to them, stopping at the end of Shane's bed. Obviously, they'd had a happy reunion. I wasn't sure how much she'd told him about recent events.

"How much do you remember about what happened before you... before you fell asleep?" I asked.

"If you're asking whether I remember being the main course at a vampire potluck dinner, the answer is yes," he

148

quipped. "Kind of hard to forget something like that. Mercifully I passed out at some point. I understand you arrived and stopped them just before they polished me off. Thank you, by the way."

"*Please* don't thank me. It's my fault you were even in that situation in the first place. I feel terrible."

"It's not your fault," he said. "That creepy 'mom' of yours is the one who told all those vamps to dig in and wished them, 'bon appetit.'"

"I know. I'm so sorry. So... I guess you also realize you were bitten multiple times?"

"Yeah. Not nearly as much fun as when I was bitten before." He slid a flirty glance at Marjorie, and she giggled.

"I lost count at about bite eight," he said.

"And you shared your blood with me three times when we were together," Marjorie reminded him.

The number of bites didn't really matter since the one Reece gave him sealed the deal.

"You should know you were on the verge of death when Reece bit you—he was the guy who was with me that day in the clinic when I had to leave. He was trying to save your life," I added.

Shane held up both hands. "Hey, it worked. Tell him thanks for me."

"Sure. I will. Of course."

Now came the hard part—making sure Shane understood what it all meant. His eyes were lilac-colored, the tell-tale sign of vampirism. But I didn't know if he felt any different.

"So..." I began.

Shane jumped in and prevented me from having to say it. "So... I guess I got a little makeover while I was sleeping, huh?"

"You look amazing," Marjorie reassured him as she reached for his hand again.

He did indeed look good. In addition to the lilac eyes, Shane seemed to have grown overnight. His shoulders looked wider, his arms were thicker and more muscular. His skin was completely clear.

"Don't worry. If you... well, if this is going to be your new life, I'll make sure there are people to guide you through the adjustment period," I said.

He pulled Marjorie closer. "Someone's already volunteered on a full-time basis." The two of them beamed at each other and shared a brief kiss.

"Good. That's great." I meant it. It was incredible to see Shane this happy. Thank God Reece hadn't let him die.

"I *was* going to suggest another option for you, but I don't know, you seem so okay with this that maybe I shouldn't even mention it."

"What option? *Two* full-time mentors?" he said. "You're welcome to join Team Help-Shane-Get-Up-To-Speed."

Marjorie didn't look quite as open to that possibility. Her brow wrinkled and she glanced between me and Shane furtively. Of course, she had no way of knowing I was deeply in love with someone else and felt only friendship toward the love of her life.

"Actually, I was going to tell you it's possible there's a cure," I said. "My friend Larkin brought it here with her. You could have it—if you want to reverse the process."

Shane was already shaking his head no before I finished making the offer.

"I'm *so* good with the way things are. I told you before I even knew Marjorie was here that I'd be okay with turning, remember? Now, I can't think of anything better than spending forever with this girl. No offense—though I don't think you were ever actually interested in me that way."

I gave him an apologetic smile. "Not really. No offense."

We all laughed.

"There *was* a time when I thought we might make a good couple," he said. "That was before I saw you with that bodyguard of yours, and I realized nothing and no one could come between the two of you."

Only my fear and sense of inadequacy.

Shane smiled at Marjorie. "I recognized it because I've felt that way before—about this beautiful person right here. I made the mistake of letting her go and not fighting for us with every breath in my body. When you've got love—the *real* thing—you shouldn't let it go for anything."

An image of Reece popped into my mind. His shirtless body stretched across my bed, the sheets bunched around his waist. The pure love in his eyes when he looked at me.

Everything I do—everything I've done since I came here was about the chance to be with you.

Reece and I *had* the real thing. He'd fought for me every step of the way, and I was going to fight for him. I wouldn't let anything stand in our way—not my fear and not the rules of the Crimson Court. Whether or not Larkin's formula worked, there were going to be some big changes around here.

Hooking my thumb over my shoulder, I took a step toward the door. "I should get going, and I'm sure you two still have a lot of catching up to do. Let me know if you need anything."

When I stepped out into the hallway, I almost bumped into Dr. Coppa.

"Oh, Abbi. I was coming to talk to you. Imogen's showing signs of coming out of it. She'll wake soon. I thought you'd want to know."

My knees went wobbly, and I had to brace one hand against the wall. Dr. Coppa's eyes said what his words had not. *I thought you'd want to know in case you want to get a head start.*

But I wouldn't be running from this. I had to face what I'd done head-on. I had publicly challenged the queen's authority. I had *privately* caused Reece to break his Bloodbound vows. And I had very possibly ended Imogen's vampire existence.

Entering her quiet room, I nodded to Kannon, who stood guard. Larkin was there too. Dr. Coppa must have notified her as well so she could see first-hand whether her research and hard work had paid off. I slipped into the chair at Imogen's bedside.

Her eyes were still closed. If she was no longer a vampire, it didn't show. She was still beautiful and unnaturally young looking. She seemed tiny under the plain white bedsheet, vulnerable, and in this state, she looked almost innocent.

It couldn't have been further from the truth, but it made me wonder once again how she had become so depraved and vindictive. She couldn't have been born that way. No one was.

When had Imogen decided power at any cost was worth so much more than peace?

If she had truly been the mother-figure I'd first taken her for, I could have asked. As it stood, the only thing I was likely to hear from her mouth when she woke was, "Off with her head."

If she was still a vampire, and therefore still queen of the Crimson Court, she was sure to order my swift execution. Larkin's and Reece's and possibly Kannon's, too.

If she had returned to her human state, it would mean the cure worked and it was possible to reverse vampirism.

It would also mean the Bastion would need a new leader and the vampire species a new queen.

There was motion in the bed. I stood, and Kannon and Larkin both came to stand at my side, all of us looking down on Imogen now, wondering, and waiting to learn our fate.

Imogen opened her eyes.
We had our answer.

* * *

THANK you for reading Crimson Bond. I hope you loved it and you're eager for more Crimson! The story concludes with Crimson Crown, available now on all ebook retailers and in paperback and coming soon to audiobook!

Turn the page for a look at the cover and a preview.

NEXT IN SERIES

CRIMSON CROWN

The Crimson Court is at a turning point, and Abigail Byler's life is about to change profoundly... or end for good. It remains to be seen what will become of the vampire queen, Imogen. And Abbi's eternal love Reece faces the possibility of taking on a job he was never meant to have while living without the only girl he's ever loved.

In this fourth and final installment of the Crimson Accord series, the fate of both the vampire and human races is at stake, and it all depends upon *who* will wear the Crimson Crown.

Don't miss the exciting conclusion of Abbi's story! Grab your copy now to find out how it all ends.

AFTERWORD

Thank you so much for reading Crimson Bond, the third book in my brand new Crimson Accord series. I hope you enjoyed it! If you did, I'd be so grateful if you'd leave a review on the retailer where you purchased it. And if your fingers aren't too tired, on Goodreads as well. It's not hard to do— just a few words about what you thought of the book is perfectly fine. Reviews are so important for authors and help other readers find great books.

The series continues with book four, Crimson Crown available now!

Members of my VIP mailing list receive fun freebies as well as notifications whenever I have new books available. Members also get sneak peeks ahead of time plus a free book just for signing up. I'd love to have you join! Here's where to do that: https://bit.ly/APsVIPs

And be sure to turn the page to check out my completed bestselling Hidden Saga series— perfect for a magical, emotional, deeply romantic book binge. For a limited time, the ebook of book 1 Hidden Deep is FREE!

THE COMPLETE CRIMSON ACCORD SERIES

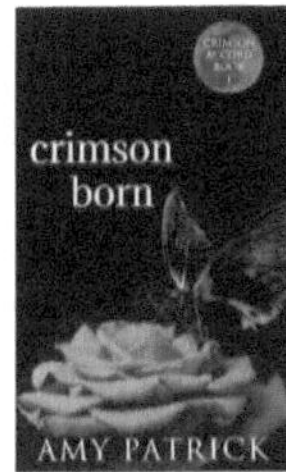

Reading order:

Crimson Born

Crimson Storm

Crimson Bond

Crimson Crown

ABOUT THE AUTHOR

Amy Patrick writes "unique" and "engrossing" (Examiner. com) romantic fiction and young adult fantasy/paranormal books that make you want to "read straight through the night into the breaking hours of dawn." (Bitten By Books)

Her hugely popular Hidden Saga is now joined by her new Crimson Accord series, a young adult vampire romance saga.

Follow Amy on Bookbub to receive notices about her new releases and sales, and join her VIP mailing list at https://bit.ly/APsVIPs for the latest book news, insider info, and fun freebies.

Amy is a multi-award-winning author and two-time RWA Golden Heart finalist and lives in Rhode Island where she enjoys writing at the beach year round. She's been a professional singer, voiceover artist, and TV news anchor, and currently writes fiction full time as well as narrating audiobooks.

Keep in touch with Amy Patrick on Facebook, Goodreads, Bookbub, Instagram and TikTok!

For more, visit her website: amypatrickbooks.com